DOCTOR'S BORDERS

Fargo was ready to storm the door when a shotgun blast opened up a huge hole in the middle of the pine slab. "You get out of here, mister!" yelled the doc. "I give you any help at all, the Sister'll burn my house down. Now you take that girl and get the hell out of here."

Fargo decided that he could probably fake the old doc out. He crept around the back of the house. Fargo began pelting the back door with the heaviest rocks he could find. The doc responded with more buckshot, putting the same size holes in the back door as he had in the front. Fargo knew he had to be patient to keep up the ruse.

Once he believed that he'd convinced the doc that he was trying to get in the back way, Fargo hurried around front and took the chance of smashing in the door with his shoulder. He stood several yards from the door, put his head down, scraped his boots against the patch of earth that led to the house, and charged.

Firt thing: the door was a hell of a lot more formidable than Fargo had estimated.

Second thing: the old doc *was* on to his plan. He'd taken up his shotgun again and started blasting away the moment he heard Fargo's shoulder hit the door.

Third thing: because the door was collapsing inward just as he was firing, the doc's shots missed Fargo by two feet.

THE
TRAILSMAN
#274

NEBRASKA
NIGHTMARE

by

Jon Sharpe

A SIGNET BOOK

SIGNET
Published by New American Library, a division of
Penguin Group (USA) Inc., 375 Hudson Street,
New York, New York 10014, U.S.A.
Penguin Books Ltd, 80 Strand,
London WC2R 0RL, England
Penguin Books Australia Ltd, 250 Camberwell Road,
Camberwell, Victoria 3124, Australia
Penguin Books Canada Ltd, 10 Alcorn Avenue,
Toronto, Ontario, Canada M4V 3B2
Penguin Books (NZ), cnr Airborne and Rosedale Roads,
Albany, Auckland 1310, New Zealand

Penguin Books Ltd, Registered Offices:
80 Strand, London WC2R 0RL, England

First published by Signet, an imprint of New American Library,
a division of Penguin Group (USA) Inc.

First Printing, August 2004
10 9 8 7 6 5 4 3 2 1

The first chapter of this book originally appeared in *Montana Massacre,* the
two hundred seventy-third volume in this series.

Copyright © Penguin Group (USA), Inc., 2004
All rights reserved

 REGISTERED TRADEMARK—MARCA REGISTRADA

Printed in the United States of America

PUBLISHER'S NOTE
This is a work of fiction. Names, characters, places, and incidents either are the
product of the author's imagination or are used fictitiously, and any resemblance
to actual persons, living or dead, events, or locales is entirely coincidental.

BOOKS ARE AVAILABLE AT QUANTITY DISCOUNTS WHEN USED TO PROMOTE
PRODUCTS OR SERVICES. FOR INFORMATION PLEASE WRITE TO PREMIUM MAR-
KETING DIVISION, PENGUIN GROUP (USA) INC., 375 HUDSON STREET, NEW YORK,
NEW YORK 10014.

The Trailsman

Beginnings . . . they bend the tree and they mark the man. Skye Fargo was born when he was eighteen. Terror was his midwife, vengeance his first cry. Killing spawned Skye Fargo, ruthless, cold-blooded murder. Out of the acrid smoke of gunpowder still hanging in the air, he rose, cried out a promise never forgotten.

The Trailsman they began to call him all across the West: searcher, scout, hunter, the man who could see where others only looked, his skills for hire but not his soul, the man who lived each day to the fullest, yet trailed each tomorrow. Skye Fargo, the Trailsman, the seeker who could take the wildness of a land and the wanting of a woman and make them his own.

Nebraska, 1860—
Let he who stands without sin cast the first stone,
let he who fires the first shot fire true—
for when the Trailsman comes to town,
final judgment arrives with better aim than most.

1

If Skye Fargo had learned one thing in all his travels, it was that trouble waited for you in the most unexpected places.

Take tonight. A pleasant early October evening near the town of Gladville, Nebraska. The smoky smell of autumn in the timberland surrounding the valley. Fargo wanted a real bath and a real bed for the simple reason that he'd gone too long without them. He was coming off the tail end of a cattle drive that had not gone well, thanks to a power-mad cattle baron who had been under the mistaken impression that hired hands were his personal slaves.

Peace and quiet tonight and then some whiskey, women and song tomorrow. He'd always heard that Gladville was a wide-open town.

As he came down the steep, rocky hill that led to the trail that would eventually take him to the town, he saw what he first thought was a bundle of rags glowing white in the moonlight. Something dropped accidentally from a Conestoga, maybe. Or somebody just throwing some old clothes away.

The rags lay next to the trail, so he had to pass them on his way into town. He took notice when the rags rolled over with no help from the windless night. Rags didn't just roll over of their own accord, now did they?

He dropped from his big Ovaro stallion, jerked his Colt from its holster and moved closer for a look-see.

A young woman. But he couldn't see much; her still-pretty face had been beaten on with considerable force.

He eased up to her. This could always be some kind of trap. Somebody hiding in the nearby timber with the girl as a lure. The facial bruises applied with dirt.

His gaze roamed the timber around him. He searched for any sign of another human being. He listened for sounds, too. But there was nothing to indicate that anybody else was around.

He went back to his stallion and grabbed his canteen. When he had raised the girl up sufficiently, he tipped the mouth of the canteen to her lips. Her blue eyes fluttered open. Her shriek was so unexpected that he damn near dropped both the canteen and the girl.

She struggled to get away, but the gouge in the back of her head sapped her strength.

"Calm down," he said gently. "I'm going to help you. But you have to help me, too. You need water and then you need a doc."

Every few moments, her entire body would jerk with pain. Then she raised a hand as if in entreaty, and fell back in his grasp. She was unconscious—or dead.

Fargo had the eerie sense he was entering a ghost town. A place named Gladville should greet visitors with the open arms of harlots and open bottles of good whiskey.

Here and there on either side of the trail he saw a light or two in one of the tiny huddled houses that made up the residential parts of the place. But the business area was dark and silent in a way that was almost sullen. None of the places that advertised themselves as saloons were open.

He was looking for a doctor's sign anywhere. With her wounds, the girl needed medical attention immediately. It took him several long minutes to find one. There, down near the river that ran from east to west, he found a yard sign that said MEDICAL DOCTOR. A small white house with a picket fence; a nice new buggy next to a shanty that housed it; and a single horse. No lights. But Fargo wasn't discouraged. No lights simply meant that the doc was probably getting some well-deserved sleep.

By this time, the girl was delirious. She moaned and wailed like a creature of the supernatural as she lay against the tree where Fargo had propped her up.

Fargo opened the gate in the picket fence and went up to the door of the house. He knocked loudly enough to be heard but not so loudly as to irritate the doc. He had to knock several times before he got any response. And the response he got was neither what he wanted or expected.

Instead of coming to the door, a short man in a nightshirt carried a small lantern to the front window and peeked out at Fargo. A nimbus of white hair gave him a fatherly look his crabbed facial features belied.

"Who are you?" the elderly doctor demanded in a squeaky voice.

"Who are *you*?" Fargo demanded back.

"Doc Mathers."

"My name's Fargo. Got a girl here who's dying. She needs help bad."

"Who is she?"

"I don't know—and what the hell's the difference? She needs a doc."

The old man cursed but he came out onto the small wooden slab of porch. He was barefooted. Fargo had spread his blanket on the ground and settled the girl on top of it.

The doc followed Fargo over to the insensate

woman, held his lantern down to her face and said, "Holy hell."

"What?"

"I can't help you, feller."

"Why the hell not?"

"Because the Sister put the word out on her. Nobody's s'posed to help Jenna Connolly."

"I don't give a damn. This girl needs help and you're going to give it to her. You're a doc."

"Don't docs have a right to refuse patients?"

"Not this doc and not this girl."

Then both doc and lantern disappeared, leaving Fargo confused and angry. What kind of doc would turn away a dying patient? And why had he declined to offer his services only after he saw the girl?

This time, Fargo pounded on the door with both fists. Each time he paused, he could hear the girl wailing again in that ghostly voice of hers.

He then took to shouting. "I don't want to bust open this door, Doc, but I will if you don't come out here right now."

He tried this three times—sounding like the big bad wolf—and then backed up several yards and canted just to the right so that his shoulder would hit the door just above the knob, popping it open.

He was ready to storm the door when a shotgun blast opened up a huge hole in the middle of the pine slab. "You get out of here, mister!" yelled the doc. "I give you any help at all, the Sister'll burn my house down. Now you take that girl and get the hell out of here."

Who the hell was this "Sister"? And why would anybody kill the doc for doing his duty? What the hell was going on in this town? First the saloons being closed up tight way before midnight. And now a doc who refused to help a dying girl because he was afraid somebody would kill him.

4

The girl had started wailing again and it unnerved Fargo. He felt so helpless. She was going to slip into death and there wasn't a damn thing he could do about it. Only the little old man inside could help her. And he didn't have long to do it.

Fargo decided that he could probably fake the old doc out. He crept around to the back of the house. The horse that was bedded down in the shanty for the night made all the noise Fargo had hoped. Wake a horse in the middle of the night and he's likely to do some complaining. The doc—unless he was stone deaf—was likely to hear it, which was exactly what Fargo wanted.

Fargo began pelting the back door with the heaviest rocks he could find. The doc responded with more buckshot, putting the same size holes in the back door as he had in the front. Fargo knew he had to be patient to keep up this ruse. He continued to pelt the back wall and the back door with anything he could find. The doc switched to some kind of handgun. Neither the bark of the gun nor the holes in the door were so dramatic anymore but the old fart kept at it.

Once he believed that he'd convinced the doc that he was trying to get in the back way, Fargo hurried around front and took the chance of smashing in the door with his shoulder as he'd originally planned.

He stood several yards from the door, put his head down, scraped his boots against the patch of earth that led to the house and charged.

First thing: the door was a hell of a lot more formidable than Fargo had estimated. Or maybe it was just the way he hit it. Either way, he was going to have one hell of a bruise on that shoulder in short order.

Second thing: the old doc *was* on to his plan. He'd taken up his shotgun again and started blasting away the moment he heard Fargo's shoulder hit the door.

Third thing: because the door was collapsing inward

just as he was firing, the doc's shots missed Fargo by two feet.

Fargo, angry, confused and needing very badly to put some hurt on this old bastard, did not slow down when he got inside the house. He dove straight for the old man, grabbing him around the middle and dragging him all the way back into a table topped with many small porcelain figures that went flying, smashing against each other in midair, breaking against the wall, shattering as they hit the floor.

The doc's shotgun went flying, too. Fargo jumped to his feet and grabbed him by the front of his nightshirt. "Now you're going to help that girl, Doc, or you're going to find yourself worse off than she is now."

He jammed the barrel of his Colt against the doc's wrinkled neck to make his point.

Fargo couldn't be absolutely sure, but he had the impression that the doc had just wet himself.

While the doc worked on the woman in his back office, Fargo slept on the floor in the front room. He was a light sleeper. His Colt was on his stomach. He'd hear the doc coming and he'd be ready.

A ticking clock was the first sound he was aware of when he woke—a small decorative clock on the living room mantel. It was nearly five in the morning.

He was on his feet, then he rushed to the other room where he found a rolltop desk and a bookcase filled with medical tomes. The doc had his head down on the writing surface of the desk. He was snoring. But he must have been a light sleeper, too; he jerked awake before Fargo was even three steps into the office.

"She's on my table in there," the doc said. "She's dead." He looked up at Fargo with an almost childlike terror in his eyes. "And now thanks to you that damned Sister's gonna come after me. Her and her gunnies."

"What're you talking about?" Fargo demanded.

"Go to that front window and take a look outside."

The odd way the old doc was carrying on, Fargo expected him to say there were ghosts waiting out there. Fargo decided to have a look, anyway. Humor the old guy.

He went to the window and slipped back the curtain. At first, he thought he was seeing an optical illusion. The three people wore capes and cowls, like monks. Their attire was so dark, it fitted into the night seamlessly, so that they seemed to be one with the darkness itself. They were spooky enough to raise Fargo's hackles.

"Who're they?"

"You stay in this town long enough, you'll find out. And they sure ain't gonna like it that you brought her here. I took care of one of the people they worked over and the next night while I was out on a call, somebody broke in here and destroyed my place. I don't want to tangle with them folks again. They sure hated that girl you brought in."

"Why?"

"Because she and her sister stood up to them."

"You think they did this to the girl?"

"I ain't sayin'. It's none of my business. And you can't make me say it." The old doc sounded like he was about five years old. He was terrified.

Fargo watched the three figures as they in turn watched him. Their faces were lost in the folds and shadows of their cowls. He couldn't even be sure of their gender. Just three dark figures standing there watching.

"Maybe I'll go talk to 'em."

"Won't do you no good. They won't talk to you. Not them. They's special. Them that wear those hoods. They're like them priests that take the vow of silence. Won't say a word to nobody."

Fargo had the sense that he'd stepped inside a bad dream. "Where's the law in all this?"

The old doc snorted. "The law? That's somethin' else you'll need to find out for yourself."

"There's a sheriff, isn't there?"

"There's a feller that wears a badge, if that's what you mean. Used to be the finest lawman I ever knew. But not no more."

Fargo let the curtain fall back in place. Then he went and got the girl and carried her outside to his stallion. He kept her wrapped warm in his blanket. He knew she was dead, but keeping her warm was just something he wanted to do. The three cowled figures watched silently.

2

By day, Gladville looked much like any other western town. A bank, a livery, two blocks of various kinds of stores and several small shops that covered everything from dentistry to tobacco.

The people looked ordinary, too. The males ran to workers, businessmen, ranch hands and farm hands. The females ran to housewives, ranch wives and shop clerks.

The one thing that seemed strange to Fargo were the men and women who wore the red armbands. He didn't know what the armbands signified. He saw maybe six or seven of them on his way to the sheriff's office. They seemed to be observing the flow of traffic—horses, wagons, stagecoaches—and, even more intently, the people who passed by them.

They seemed friendly enough, smiling at various citizens, even lending a hand when somebody was carrying too many packages or when somebody old and infirm needed a hand to step up to the board sidewalk.

Most mystifying to Fargo were the tablets they held. Every so often, they'd write something down. It was as if they'd heard or seen something that disturbed them and they needed to document it. This seemed to give them some kind of official status. He'd never seen anything like it before.

He passed the final one—a tall, scrawny older man with a grin on his face but a certain kind of crazy anger in his dark eyes—gave a little nod and opened the door with the word SHERIFF on it.

The layout here was as familiar as the layout of the town itself. A large front room with three small desks. Wanted posters on one wall. Shotguns and rifles locked up in cases along another. A connecting door to the jail cells in back. And the smell of hard, bitter coffee that seemed to go with the job of sheriff just about everywhere.

A lone man sat at the desk in back. He had the look of a sentimental grandfather in a magazine illustration. Bushy white hair, an open and friendly smile and eyes filled with charity, compassion and neighborly interest. But he looked fatigued, spent.

"Help you?" the man said. With his blue work shirt, leather vest and good gray trousers, he had managed to keep the common touch. Except for the star he wore on his vest, he could have been a carpenter or a clerk or a farmer come to town for the day.

"I'm looking for the sheriff."

"Well, you're looking in the right place. Dave Sadler."

He offered a hard slab of hand. The men shook.

"My name's Skye Fargo."

"I've heard of you, but I don't believe I've seen you around here before."

"Just traveling through. Or at least I was until I ran into a little trouble last night."

Sadler pointed to a chair. "Well, why don't you sit down right there and tell me about it. I'll get both of us a cup of coffee. Believe it or not, bad as it smells, it actually tastes pretty good." He grinned. "Leastways, that's what people tell me when I threaten to arrest them if they don't tell me how good it is."

Fargo had never seen a lawman this lethargic. The

sheriff dragged himself around as if he were carrying a huge safe on his back. He sighed every few minutes.

The coffee was much better than expected, as promised. By the time Fargo finished his cup, his story was finished, too.

"Well, Doc Mathers is a friend of mine." Sadler studied Fargo a moment. "The Sister has him scared, just like she has the whole town scared."

"I've heard as much. Who's this Sister, anyway?"

But Fargo would have to wait for an explanation.

The front door opened. A mountain man in buckskins and an Old Testament beard came in. He wore a silver star on his shirt.

The first thing he said was, "Dave, you get those forms filled out for me yet? I'm s'posed to have 'em to the courthouse this afternoon."

The mountain man spoke in the irritable tone of a boss who finds his employee to be incompetent. But the badge the mountain man wore said DEPUTY. Deputies didn't usually speak to sheriffs that way.

"I'll have them for you, Hack," the older man said defensively. He sounded embarrassed to be called to task in front of Fargo. "By the way, Mr. Fargo, this is Hack Heller, one of my deputies."

"I actually run the place, Fargo," Heller said. He put a joking edge on it but it was clear he wasn't kidding.

The older man's cheeks bloomed red. He turned around and faced his rolltop desk.

"So what can we do for you, Fargo?" Heller said.

Fargo explained the circumstances around the woman's, Jenna Connolly's, death.

Heller said, "I'd say it sounds like the Sister but she doesn't kill people. That's the only reason that half the town hasn't gone up to that fort of hers and burned her out."

"The sheriff here was just going to tell me about her," Fargo said.

"Well, since I get around more than the sheriff does these days, I probably know a little bit more about her." Heller had turned condescension into an art form.

Sister Salvation was an itinerant preacher who claimed to be in direct touch with God, Heller explained. She was a powerful speaker and had converted half the town to her beliefs. Her people were fanatics. They believed they were morally superior by following a very severe code they claimed came directly from the Bible. The Guardians, who wore red armbands, came to town every day to keep a record of sinners and their sins. Once somebody was considered to be a serious sinner, terrible things, large and small, began happening to him or her. The adulteress found herself tied to a tree and lashed forty times with a whip. The man who paid a visit to a bawdy house had both his legs broken in a mysterious fall. The schoolmarm who refused to incorporate Sister Salvation's teachings into her lessons was driven out of town by whispers that she was a bit too intimate with anyone and everyone from other women to older students. And so on.

There was one more note of interest about the good Sister. While her religious people worked the farmland on either side of the fort, she had a cadre of ten men who were gunfighters and thieves protecting her personally. They did more than that, too. Since she'd arrived here two years ago, stagecoach and bank robberies had quadrupled. There wasn't much doubt that it was her gunnies who were responsible for the robberies. But nobody had been able to prove it.

"She's got the whole damn town scared," Heller finished. "You'll notice people hurry on their way. They don't dawdle the way they would in normal towns. They're afraid of the red armbands. You never know what's going to set those folks off. You might do something that they think is a sin—and that night, your barn burns down."

"Nobody ever stood up to her?"

Heller smirked. "Well, the sheriff here had a chance to. But he was too busy with other things to notice how strong she was gettin'. That's when the town council hired me. But I only been here two months. I'm makin' progress but it's slow." He nodded to Sadler, who was still staring straight ahead at his desk, trying to shut out the insults. "But I'm not gettin' much help, if you know what I mean."

Heller walked over and poured himself a cup of coffee. "Now if you don't mind, Fargo, Dave and me here have some business to discuss." He winked at Fargo. "Assumin' I can wake him up, that is."

He had a nasty laugh, Heller did. Almost as nasty as his ice blue eyes.

By the time she'd nailed up the first poster, Jane Connolly had an audience, three townswomen who followed her from one place to another as the young, pretty woman proved how courageous she was.

"Her sister's dead, you know," whispered one of the ladies.

"It's terrible, what this town's come to," whispered another.

"But she's going ahead with that rally, anyway," said the third.

"Wouldn't be surprised if somebody killed her to stop it," said the first.

The rally the women in their gingham bonnets and dresses were referring to was the one Jane and Jenna had announced two weeks ago. Its purpose was to get the good people of the town—those not in thrall to Sister Salvation—to stand together, like at a revival meeting, and denounce what had happened to their town.

Some people figured that with Jenna Connolly dead the rally wouldn't be held. But they hadn't counted on Jane Connolly's rage. Her sister's death had only made her angrier and more determined to see the rally through, even though several "sensible" voices in town—including Hack Heller's—had warned her that the Sister would send down a couple of gunnies to disrupt things.

Over the next half-hour, Jane Connolly put up eighteen hand-written posters. Some people smiled over how foolish she was; others remarked on how brave she was; and two of the younger men, long smitten by her, extolled her beauty.

For the next eighteen hours, anyway, Jane would be the most popular person in Gladville.

3

The folks with the red armbands had doubled in number. As the day went on, there was more and more foot traffic in town, and there had to be more red armbands to watch them.

And to fill those tablets.

Fargo watched as they walked up and down the streets. They tended to greet people with smiles but few returned the favor. The animosity between the red armbands and the average citizen was easy to see and feel.

Fargo had passed through such towns before. Crackpot religions sprang up all over the West. Some were attached to otherwise respectable churches—the crackpots were fringe members of established faiths. Others established their own faiths. Some practiced extreme forms of cruelty, especially against women and children; some practiced what seemed to be simply an excuse for some good times, especially those churches that encouraged nudity. Others were just incomprehensible, such as those that spoke in tongues and claimed to be summoned to heaven on a regular basis and then returned to earth with madness in their eyes and harsh words for their fellow man for living in sin.

The red armbands had an angry edge to them. The

smiles were cold, contemptuous. And when they saw anything they believed was worth writing down, they did so with great relish. They sure did a lot of writing. It was a wonder most of them didn't have writer's cramp by now. They seemed to see sin in the most innocent of moments.

Fargo put into a café and ordered flapjacks and bacon and a pot of coffee all his own.

He was about finished with his breakfast when the dead woman he'd brought into town last night came from nowhere and sat across from him. It took a minute for Fargo to see the difference between the dead woman and this one. It wasn't much—a small beauty mark near the left edge of her mouth. And this one had gray eyes instead of blue.

"I'm hoping you'll take a walk with me," the woman said. "I've got a gun under this table, Mr. Fargo. The mood I'm in, I'll be happy to kill you if you decline my invitation."

"Gosh, it's nice of you to be so concerned that I get my exercise."

"Let's go."

"I never could argue with a loaded gun."

He figured he wouldn't have much difficulty taking the gun away from her. The problem was that in the cramped café, the gun might misfire while he was struggling with her, and some innocent customer might get shot or even killed. The food was so bad here that he wouldn't have minded shooting the owner.

He paid for his meal and they went outside.

"It's sure fun walking down the street with a beautiful woman who has a gun pointing at you from inside her purse."

"I wish I could be as happy as you are. But I can't be, because my little sister is dead."

"Jenna?"

"Yes."

"I didn't kill her."

"Maybe not. But maybe you saw who did. I'm betting it was one of Sister Salvation's people."

They were progressing down the main street, working their way between clattering wagons and clopping horses. The mild autumn day had the effect of a miracle tonic on Fargo's spirits—he felt optimistic that he was going to find the killer both he and this woman were looking for.

As they passed one of the red armbands, the man quickly scrawled something on his tablet. "Those are the Guardians." The angry woman allowed herself a smirk. "They're something, aren't they? Sister Salvation says that they're guarding against sin. They keep track of your behavior. If they hear you swear, or do anything but say good morning to somebody who's married, or look at another person in a 'lustful' way, then they pay you a visit at home and offer to 'cleanse' you. If you don't agree to be cleansed, a lot of bad things can happen to you. It can be anything from them stealing the wheels off your wagon in the middle of the night to doing what happened to Jenna."

They were at the river. They found a bench and sat down. "I think I can trust you," she said. "I'd sure like to take my hand out of this purse. It's starting to get a cramp from holding the gun this long."

"Be my guest."

"But first you have to give me an honest answer."

"All right."

"Do you know who killed my sister?"

"No, I don't, Miss Connolly. When I saw her on the side of the road, she was unconscious and alone. I didn't see anybody else around."

She removed her hand and snapped the purse shut.

They sat for a few silent moments, looking at a barge on the big, muddy river.

"There's a steamship through here every week," the

woman said, looking pert and crisp in her blue dress with the white starched collar. "I always tried to convince Jenna to come away with me. Anywhere. But she wouldn't. She wanted to stay here and fight Sister Salvation. Jenna believed in principles. But I didn't have her courage." Her expression turned bitter. "Till now. Jenna had been planning this rally for tonight. That's why she was killed. And I'm sure of it. I'm going to make sure it goes ahead."

Jane smiled sentimentally. "She was stubborn. I'm like our mom. Try to settle everything peacefully. Jenna is—was—more like our dad. Nobody ever told him what to do, by God. He might go down but he'd go down swinging. That's just the way he was."

"And she paid the price."

She looked at the mill on the far bank of the muddy river. "This was a wide-open town before Sister Salvation came. The gambling was crooked, the violence was terrible, the whoring was unbelievable. The decent people didn't speak up. They'd have been killed if they had. The men who owned the saloons also owned the town. So when Sister Salvation came along, a lot of the good people flocked to her. She stood up to the saloons. And she made religious converts out of a lot of folks. She didn't start out with the red armbands; that came later."

"Where does she live?"

"There's this army fort. When the Indian tribes they were keeping an eye on moved further west, the fort stood empty. She paid the government a pittance for it. That's the center of her activities."

"I'll have to take a ride out there."

"Be careful. They shoot at strangers."

"Heller tells me she hasn't had anybody killed."

Tears gleamed in her eyes. "Up till when Jenna was killed, I guess that's right. Arson was more her style. But she made sure nobody died."

18

Fargo was just about to take the makings out of his shirt pocket to roll himself a cigarette when he glanced across the street and saw the man standing about twenty feet away. A man with a red armband on. A man writing in a tablet while he stared right at Fargo and Jane.

"Guess we're doing something wrong," he said. "Maybe we're breathing air that belongs to Sister Salvation."

"It's me," Jane said. "Somebody was stalking Jenna all the time. They'll come after me now. That's one of the things they do to intimidate people. Follow them around and write down everything you do. Once in a while they'll even point at you and start shouting 'Sinner! Sinner!' till everybody's watching you. It's humiliating. They did it to Jenna after she announced that she was going to hold this rally."

"I guess I should take care of a little business here," Fargo said as he stood, preparing to go over to the man who'd been watching them. "I'll talk to you later."

If Fargo made him nervous, the man didn't show it. He had righteousness on his side and no saddle tramp was going to make him cower. That was how Fargo read the expression on the man's wide, cheeky face, anyway.

"Morning," Fargo said when he reached him.

The man just looked at him.

"You ever been punched in the face?" Fargo said.

For the first time, the man looked concerned. "I don't have to talk to you."

"That's true enough," Fargo said. "But then I don't have to stand by, either, and let you write about me in your book."

"Maybe I'm not writing about you."

"Well, then how about letting me check out your book."

Before the man could even change expression, Fargo leaned forward and tore the book from his hands. Then he shoved the man about six feet backwards.

He turned and walked away. "By the way, if Sister Salvation wants to know my name, it's Skye Fargo. That's with an 'e' on the 'Skye'."

When he got back to the park bench they'd been sitting on, he said, "There's probably a lot of real dirty reading in here." He laughed. "I'm looking forward to it."

On the way back to her rooming house, Jane stopped in the middle of the main street and looked at the bench she would be standing on tonight. There certainly wasn't any merchant who would let her use their steps for her speech. She'd have to use public property. There was a small grassy entrance to the public park area, and it was there she would stand, trying to talk some common sense and some courage into the heads of her fellow townspeople.

What if nobody showed up? What if Sister Salvation's gunnies tried to break it up? What if Hack Heller forced her to stop speaking?

No. She wouldn't relent no matter what. She owed Jenna that. She owed it to herself, too. Why couldn't a woman be as principled and strong as a man? Why couldn't a woman lead a movement that would return the town to its rightful owners? Why couldn't a woman face down another woman—she was in no way afraid of Sister Salvation.

She raised the skirt of her long dress and helped herself up on the bench. The old men playing checkers paused in their game and looked over at her. "You got guts, girlie. Got to say that for you."

Everybody in town knew about the rally tonight. It would be up to her to stir them and embolden them and give them the direction they needed. She wished she had Jenna's speaking skills. Maybe she'd be so bad at it she'd be a laughingstock. Maybe they'd be simply amused, the way those two old checker players were.

One of the old men said, "You'll be gettin' a crowd tonight for sure. People always show up when there's a pretty gal to see. And you're about the prettiest gal in the valley."

Jane smiled. The old man had some fire in him even now. He was flirting with her and she found it funny and dear at the same time. If only she could find a man her age with such stamina—well, the one she'd met would fill the job well. Skye Fargo was one hard-rock specimen of man. The problem was he was a drifter. That was evident. She couldn't imagine the kind of woman it would take to get him to settle down.

But he certainly had his uses. She sensed that he'd not only be here tonight but that he also might be talked into helping her out in the early stages of taking the town back. After all, he'd been the one who'd found Jenna. And that wasn't anything a man could forget easily, especially a man like Fargo. He didn't look eager to fight but she had the feeling that once you riled him, it would be best to hide yourself in another part of the territory. Because Fargo was definitely the kind of man who'd come after you.

If only he'd agree to come after Sister Salvation. What a pleasure it would be to see her get justice.

She watched as three men with red armbands made their way over to her. They didn't look happy. Their artificial smiles were nowhere to be seen.

"Good day, Miss Connolly."

"Good day, Mr. Garner."

"Miss Connolly, Mr. Green and Mr. Heathrow here have been talking."

"I'll bet that's an interesting conversation."

"There's no need for sarcasm."

"And just what were Mr. Green and Mr. Heathrow talking *about,* Mr. Garner?"

"Why, they were talking about your safety, of course. What everybody in town is talking about."

They looked like three monkeys—see no evil, hear no evil, speak no evil—in the cheap checkered suits that drummers wore. Each also wore a derby. They were hayseeds gussied up as city slickers and there was something pathetic about them. She could almost feel sorry for them if she didn't know some of the things they'd done to the nonbelievers they'd once called friends. They now saw their old friends—people they'd been around for twenty years or more—as the devil's minions.

"Well, Mr. Garner, fortunately I'm old enough to worry about my own safety."

"Sister Salvation herself is praying for you," Mr. Green said.

"I'll bet she is."

"There's that sarcasm again, Miss Connolly," Mr. Heathrow said.

She sighed. "I'm trying to control myself here. My sister is dead. And I'm pretty sure I know who did it."

"If you're thinking it was Sister Salvation," Mr. Garner said, "you're wrong."

"You'll have to prove I'm wrong before I'll believe it. And even if Jenna wasn't dead, I'd still be holding this rally tonight because your beloved Sister Salvation has gone too far. All the hatred and pain and fear she's brought here—plus, that fort of hers is nothing more than a hideout for all the robberies she's had her thugs pull off."

Each man was spluttering and blubbering a defense of the good Sister, but Jane held up a hand and stopped them. "Can't you see that she's twisted your beliefs to her own purposes, that she's not saving you, she's using you? We've got two very good ministers right here in Gladville. Why don't you go to church with them on Sunday mornings?"

"Because they don't teach the truth," Mr. Garner snapped.

Jane couldn't help herself. Her laugh was quick and scornful. "Writing down the sins of your friends; hiding outlaws in your fortress; and maybe even killing people who speak up against you—I suppose that's the truth."

But Mr. Garner was now too angry to listen. "Terrible things could happen if you go forward with this rally tonight."

"Terrible things," Mr. Heathrow repeated.

"Then I'll have to deal with them when they do," she said coldly. "Now, if you gentlemen don't mind, I've got work to do."

They left even angrier than they'd arrived.

4

Sister Salvation (Catherine Daye) was ageless in the sense that nobody could figure out how old she was. In some attire and some light, she looked fortyish; in other attire and other light, she looked fiftyish. Whatever her age, she was still a regal, if faded, beauty.

Today as she walked around inside the fort greeting her followers and inspecting everything with the sharp and merciless eye of a general, she wore a virginal white dress which did nothing to disguise her richly formed body.

She was greeted with smiles and waves; with admiration and even awe. Her followers believed that she spoke nightly to God and that the word she shared with them was the word she herself had received. They didn't question her. How could they? She not only spoke to God—she spoke *for* Him.

They didn't know anything about her background and wouldn't have believed it if you told them. Artist's model in New York City, crib whore in New Orleans, saloon manager in Kansas City, and—thanks to the most handsome and cunning man she'd ever known—religious icon.

Griff Evans had been a faith healer when she met

him fifteen years ago. After she started traveling with him, he noticed how when she was on the platform with him, most eyes stayed on her. Especially when she sang in that sweet high trembling voice of hers. He made her the faith healer.

One thing about Griff, he always looked for ways to improve a situation. They took to inviting people to join their religious crusade. Griff would find large buildings that had been deserted and this was where the faithful would live. They would always be near farmland so they could raise their own animals and crops. They would give Sister Salvation, as she was now called, all their wordly possessions before moving in. Most of their followers were average people who didn't have much to give her. But some were rich people; they bestowed a lot. Griff added one more trick. He always hired a handful of gunnies to pretend that they were followers, too. Using the religion as their cover, they robbed banks, stagecoaches, even mansions when nobody was home.

They'd done this four times in ten years. Griff thought that the Gladville area would be the most profitable they'd been to yet. He was right. But he didn't live to see it. Griff liked his sex and Griff liked his liquor. They proved to be his downfall. He was having his way with a girl in the woods when a timber rattlesnake bit him on his bare ass. This would ordinarily be a tale for amusement to be told again and again. But Griff died from the poison and there was nothing funny about that.

She'd loved him. He'd screwed anything that walked—probably even dogs and cats, if the truth be known—he hid money from her; he even whored her out to a businessman who wanted to invest in one of Griff's fictitious "gold mine" schemes. But she loved him. All her life, she'd been told that she was a callous, mercenary, selfish bitch. She knew this to be true.

But then she had to go get all damp-palmed and damp-thighed goofy about a man like Griff.

She was tired of it all now as she walked around the fort. Tired of her own voice as she excoriated sinners; tired of the songs she'd sung to a deity she didn't believe in; and tired of reassuring frightened people there were no boogeymen she couldn't handle. People were making soap, washing clothes, tending to horses, feeding babies, making crude furniture—all the small jobs of daily life in a fort. At least this fort.

The loot from the various robberies had been divided last night. Hers filled a dozen bags that would be loaded on a wagon tonight. Tomorrow, Sister Salvation would slip away.

And just in time, too, with that damn rally still scheduled for tonight. But she wouldn't have to worry about surviving here anymore. She was taking her share and heading for San Francisco, making the trip that she and Griff had talked about for so long, but had never got around to.

Less than twenty-four hours to go with these simpering, helpless fools who believed she spoke directly to a God that probably didn't even exist.

"We've decided on a name for our baby!" cried a woman sitting in front of the tiny shed she shared with her husband and four children. "We're calling her Salvation! Naming her after you!"

Sister Salvation dredged up a weary smile and said, "Well, isn't that just dandy?"

Hack Heller sat his horse in the hills to the east of Sister Salvation's fort. He had finally decided how he and his outlaw friend Decker would get the loot from the locked shed inside the fort.

He lifted his field glasses again. Inside the fort, two men were sweeping out a wagon of their own. The wagon stood near the back gate of the fort. Heller was going to steal the wagon and load it up with the loot from the good Sister's various robberies.

Heller, hungry, turned his horse back toward home.

5

One of the Guardians had spent twenty minutes telling Sister Salvation what he'd learned in town this morning. She told him to find Kate Doyle and bring her here.

The Guardian found Kate showing her sister, Molly, how to use the washboard. Kate had lustrous dark hair and a slender body. She also had eyes so dark they were startling the first time you saw them.

Molly was "teched" or "slow," as most people chose to call it. She'd been struck by lightning ten years earlier and hadn't been right since. She could barely form a sentence, rarely remembered something she'd learned an hour earlier and was given to weeping so inconsolably it was frightening to watch. Her body was a shapeless mass and her face a balloon dotted with tiny features. The girls had lost their parents four years ago in a riverboat accident. Her only recent pleasure was a kitten she'd followed around—a white one with a black ring around one eye.

Kate sought religion as the only way she could make peace with her troubled life. But she wanted a religion that gave her a catharsis at least once a day. She wanted to stay drunk on it. The ordinary religions offered no such thrill. But Sister Salvation—Kate could get so high she was barely aware of what she was doing.

She stood before Sister Salvation now, a supplicant of the most fervent kind.

Sister Salvation poured them tea and they sat at a small table next to an open window. Autumn was radiant in sight and scent alike.

"I need you to do something for me, Kate."

"Of course, Sister."

"You know about the rally in town tonight."

"The devil's work."

"Indeed it is, Kate. It needs to be stopped."

"They won't stop it now that Jenna Connolly's died."

"They think I killed her."

"They're liars, Sister."

"Yes, they are." She hesitated. "I've been told that Jane Connolly has a new friend. A man named Skye Fargo. I want you to go talk to him and ask him to get the rally canceled. For everybody's sake. I don't want people to get hurt. And crowds can get pretty angry sometimes." Her concern was simple. If the crowd got angry enough, they might come out here and surround the fort. How would she get away with her loot if that happened?

"I'd better change my clothes."

"Wear your Sunday dress. You look very pretty in it."

"Yes, Sister."

She took the young woman's hand. "Do what you need to get him on your side, Kate."

Kate was obviously shocked. "You don't mean—"

"Lives are at stake, Kate. The Lord will understand if you stray from the path in a case like this. You'll be doing His work."

Kate could think of nothing but the Sister's final words. Maybe she had misinterpreted what the holy woman said—surely she couldn't have meant *giving* herself to this man called Fargo. . . . But the Sister's words were soon forgotten, because when she found Molly she had to tell her about her trip into town.

"I won't be gone long," Kate said, hugging her sister tight. "And you'll be fine here. Just ask Lem if you need anything."

That was as far as she got. Molly began weeping. Kate spent half an hour consoling her. Then it was time to get ready for town and leave.

Her last image of Molly was of a round face looking sad, silly and lost all at the same time. She felt guilty about leaving poor Molly. But how could she disobey the Sister?

6

Fargo had logged three hours of sleep before the tiny knock woke him. He had his Colt in its holster strapped to the bedpost. It filled his hand now.

"Who is it?"

"I need to clean your room. I'm the owner's daughter."

"You got a key?"

"Uh, yeah."

"Well, I don't have any clothes on but I'm under the blanket so you come in and clean and I'll just stay in bed."

"Well, I guess that'll be all right."

She turned out to be a tiny redhead who didn't lack for curves or a glint of humor in the eyes that belied the hesitant voice. She wore britches and a man's blue workshirt that did mighty fine things for her chest. She was probably about twenty.

"I haven't dusted in here in a while."

"I guess I don't notice things like that."

"Well, I'll be as quiet as I can be. You go on back to sleep. I'll just dust a little and pick things up a bit and then get out of here."

He went to sleep with one eye but stayed wide awake with the other. It was that eye that watched as the small girl stood on tiptoes to dust. Those britches did awfully admirable things to her perfectly shaped buttocks.

When she turned around again, she saw it right away. True to the hint of merriment in her eyes, she didn't blush. She smiled. "You have a tent pole under there?"

"That's all me, darlin'."

"Looks kinda funny, actually."

"I trained it to do that."

She smiled. "I'll just bet you did. I'll bet you trained it a lot."

"And right now—I'm not absolutely sure about this but I'm pretty sure—right now I think it could use a little more training."

"It could, huh?"

"Yep. I believe it could."

"Maybe I could spiff it up a little for you."

"Well, that would be right neighborly of you, miss."

"Sort of dust it up a little."

"You know, I think that's right. I think it *could* use a good dustin' now that you mention it."

"Sort of like this?"

She walked over to the bed and pulled the blanket back, then took her dust cloth and began to buff up the proud stout symbol of his manhood. He squealed and writhed and made fists of his hands, the pleasure was so great. This was one little gal who sure knew how to use a dust cloth.

He had never seen anybody get out of her clothes with the speed she did. One moment she was standing next to the bed, the next she was crawling, completely naked, over his body so that she could straddle him.

Fargo—you didn't get any sex on a cattle drive, so it had been a while—Fargo damned near lost his vision and his voice when she guided his shaft up the warm juicy insides of her sex and began riding him with merciless and mind-boggling skill. She had small but young, firm breasts and nipples so sensitive that she got as hot and bothered as he was the moment he touched them.

She approached what became a series of explosive climaxes almost as soon as he gripped her small buttocks in his massive hands. Not that this slowed her down any. She attacked his mouth with her tongue, raising his fever and frenzy even higher.

Without any warning, she flung herself off him and off the bed and turned away from him so that she could bend over the bureau and he could ride her from the rear. Her womanhood was as tight and tender and deliciously hot as it had been in their other position. He drove himself again and again, harder and deeper inside her. She began tossing her head from side to side, as if she simply couldn't endure this kind of blinding glee.

He felt her slender legs shaking badly. She was ready to collapse under his onslaught. His thrusts filled her to capacity, so that when he peaked, he was for a long exhilarating moment one with his own tidal wave of pleasure. After he eased himself out, he lifted her up and carried her to the bed, where he dumped her with a laugh. "That's a lot better than collapsing on the floor."

They both spoke in ragged gasps, out of breath. "It's as if you're planning to get in here with me," she said.

"I'm just rolling myself a cigarette."

"Roll me one while you're at it."

"I didn't think proper young ladies were supposed to smoke."

"I'll give you a hint—I mean in case you haven't figured it out by now—I haven't been proper for a day in my life."

"You mean the sex? You're damn good. *Damn* good."

"So are you, handsome. But that isn't what I was talking about."

"Oh? I'm not following you."

She smiled with white, sweet, cute little teeth. "I'm not the maid, you dummy. I have a room down the hall. When I saw you come in, I knew right away I had to have you. So I convinced the desk clerk to give me the skeleton key. I told him it was your birthday and I wanted to surprise you."

"If you're not the maid, who are you?"

"A schoolmarm. I'm here for a conference this weekend. Some fella from Lincoln is supposed to teach us how to be better teachers."

Fargo finished rolling them cigarettes and went over and stretched out on the bed next to her. "They sure don't make teachers the way they used to."

Ken Granger was the head of the town council and one of Sheriff Sadler's oldest friends. Sadler had noticed that these days, Granger always seemed uncomfortable, even embarrassed.

Sadler was just coming out of the café when he spotted Granger, who instantly looked for an escape route. But since they were less than ten feet apart, it would look damn funny if Granger suddenly cut and ran, pretending not to have seen the sheriff.

"Hey there, Ken," Sadler said, drumming up a cheery sound, though he wasn't feeling cheery at all.

"Good to see you," Granger said, pumping Sadler's hand as if he was a politician soliciting a vote. Granger was a short, squat, powerfully constructed man whose usual good nature had made him and his stage line a lot of friends.

"Say, I'm still waiting for that supper invitation, old friend."

"Well, darned if Mae wasn't reminding me of that just last night. We'll pick a date and I'll tell you about it."

Then the inevitable subject. Sadler said: "Tim

Haines over at the hardware store, he said there was a secret council meeting last night."

Granger scowled. "What's the point of having secret meetings if everybody talks about them?"

"He told me that Hack Heller was making some jokes about me."

There, it was said. Heller had been making jokes about him for weeks and Haines had been telling Sadler about them—not the jokes themselves, nor even a specific reference to Sadler. But the way he put it—"He sure does like to make fun of people behind their backs"—it was pretty obvious what he was talking about.

Granger's brown eyes began earnestly studying the ground. "Dave, none of us likes the way this's worked out. But between your wife dyin' and Sister Salvation takin' over half the town—well, it just seems you don't have your old gumption. I mean, neither one of us is exactly a spring chicken. And Heller—" He sighed. "Heller's the kind of man we need right now. He keeps Sister Salvation's people to a minimum. Hell, he runs those so-called Guardians out three times a week."

"They come back. Same as they did when I was runnin' things."

"Yeah, but there ain't as many of them and they sure scatter when Heller's on the warpath. Same as her holdin' those Bible meetings of hers. Heller's got 'em out in the boonies now. They used to be right here in town and they wouldn't budge." He looked as miserable as Sadler felt. He put a hand on Sadler's shoulder and said, "I was careful to see that you stayed on as the sheriff."

"In name only, Ken. He's got me doin' all his paperwork. Like I'm his secretary or somethin'."

Granger shook his head. "The town council knows what Hack is—he's just as much of a crook and a gunny as anybody the Sister's got workin' for her. But right now he's the most effective weapon we got. They're scared of him, Dave."

"And they aren't afraid of me?"

Granger sighed. "Aw, Dave. You're about the most decent man I've ever known. And I don't mean 'decent' in that pious way the Sister puts on. You're kind, you help people, you were never trigger happy and you were honest. But—times are different now, Dave. That's the only way I can say it." He nodded to some spot down the street. "I need to be going now. But I'll be back to you in the next couple of days. We'll have that dinner. It'll be just like the old days, Dave.

He gave a salute off the edge of his derby brim and walked on.

Sadler stood there, shoulders slumped, a faint glistening on his eyes. Then he shook his head. "The old days."

7

When Sadler looked up and said, "Oh, it's you, Fargo," Fargo thought he'd never seen a man that sad.

"You all right?"

"For a useless old fart who's sheriff in name only, I'm doing just fine. Excuse the self-pity."

"Self-pity is fun sometimes. I go for a swim in it every once in a while. You just have to be careful not to drown in it."

Sadler sat up in his swivel chair and said, "I guess that's a good point." He looked at the papers on his desk. "Being Heller's secretary kinda gets me down sometimes. Or maybe you hadn't noticed that Hack is the real sheriff around here?"

Fargo said, "May I have some coffee?"

"Sure."

After he had coffee in hand, Fargo walked back and leaned against the wall. "Yeah, I guess I noticed that: how Heller seems to make all the decisions."

"Well, he's welcome to all of it. I'm going to pack up and leave town."

"That what you really want to do?"

Sadler smiled. "No, Fargo. If I did what I really wanted to do, they'd be hanging me from that gallows down the street by the courthouse."

Fargo laughed. "Now, would doing what you want to do involve Hack Heller and a six-gun and then Heller spending the night over at the mortuary?"

"Yeah, somethin' like that. But I've been wallowing long enough. Like you say, a man has to be careful. Self-pity can get downright dangerous sometimes." He looked at Fargo and sat up even straighter in his chair. "So let's pretend I'm really the sheriff. So what is it I can do for you, feller?"

"You can tell me about David Caine."

"You mean you want to know more than that he's a slippery character who went through his own inheritance and is now tryin' everything he can to get his sister's?"

"I didn't know about the sister. But he sure did strike me as slippery." Fargo reached into his back pocket and tossed the money on Sadler's desk. "He hired me. That's five hundred dollars you're looking at there."

"What's he want you to do?"

"He says he wants me to find out who killed Jenna Connolly. Claims he was in love with her."

Sadler snorted. "He tried to have sex with her. Which wasn't any special thing where he's concerned. He's tried to have sex with every woman—married or unmarried—in town. Someday, some husband is gonna stave in his head for him."

"So why did he hire me?"

"My guess is all I can give you."

"That's why I came here. You're the sheriff."

"Well," Sadler said, grinning. "Sorta."

"That's good enough for me."

Sadler reached over and chose a pipe from a small rack of them. "The way I see it is that he wants you to find out if his sister Helen did it."

"Why would she do it?"

"Jenna used to work for her husband. There were whispers all over town that they spent a lot of time together after-hours."

"So it's at least a possibility that Helen might have done it?"

"It's at least a possibility, yes. Her husband, Evan, is also a possibility. I heard he was ready to leave Helen for Jenna but Jenna backed out. She couldn't handle the scandal."

"So you can't rule them out as suspects?"

"Nope. Both Helen and Evan Chandler would have reasons to kill her. But there's one other thing."

"What's that?"

"If it's Helen, there's a chance David could bribe some judge to let him take over Helen's inheritance. And if it's Evan—well, David would be beside himself. He resents the influence Evan has on Helen. With Evan out of the way, David would have his sister all to himself. He could probably go through her inheritance about as fast as he went through his own."

"So he doesn't want the killer to be Sister Salvation?"

"If it's Sister Salvation, Fargo, he doesn't get anything out of it. And David doesn't like to do anything that doesn't come out in his favor."

Fargo finished his coffee. "Well, I'm going back to my hotel room and then down to see Helen Chandler." He laughed. "You've got a lot of interesting people in this town, Sheriff."

"You should've been here in the old days. A couple of murders every weekend or so. There were a lot of interesting folks here back then."

"That sounds a little *too* interesting to me," Fargo said. "I like a little peace and quiet."

"The Trailsman? Peace and quiet? That sounds pretty far-fetched to me."

"So do most of the stories I hear about myself,"

Fargo said. "They keep the dime novelists busy. But they don't have much to do with reality."

He went over and put his tin coffee cup back. "I'll let you know how I come out with Helen Chandler."

"Yeah," Sadler said, sounding intrigued. "The hell of it is, Helen's a nice woman. But you sure don't want to cross her. She can really get crazy sometimes."

Fargo grinned. "I'll tell her you said that."

"You do that, Fargo, and she won't invite me to her birthday party any more. And that's about the biggest social event in town."

Kate always felt sinful when she was in town. She one day hoped to cleanse herself of all selfish and petty desires. Who cared about pretty dresses and hats? Who cared about sparkly baubles and Parisian perfume? Who cared about pleasures of the flesh?

Well, the heck of it was, Kate cared. And so on those occasions when Sister Salvation sent her into town, every selfish, greedy, impure thought Kate had ever had sprang to mind again. Just passing down the row of women's stores was enough to make her feel deliciously wicked and admit to herself that she really didn't much enjoy her life at the fort. And after Sister Salvation told her this morning that there were times—all in the name of serving the Lord, of course—when it was all right to give yourself to a man . . . her doubts about the whole enterprise at the fort came to the fore.

But then her religious training would make itself felt. She would excoriate herself for giving in to Satan. That's who had planted all those doubts in her mind. That's who put those urges and longings in her body. That's who urged her to flee to a town and lead a sinful life.

But now that she was in town, she allowed herself to enjoy the clutter and clamor of the main street. The pretty women. The handsome men. The elegant shops—at least to her untutored eye they looked elegant.

She decided to treat herself to a lemonade at the general store. Even that made her feel deliciously decadent. She turned over and over the good Sister's words . . . could she really have meant what it sounded as if she meant? About Kate giving herself? My Lord. . . .

8

Fargo was ready to kill whoever waited for him behind his hotel room door, but when he saw that his
intruder was a beautiful young woman, he put his
gun away and smiled. He slammed the door behind
him. The sound was so violent, the girl jerked in
her chair.

"Kind of a dangerous thing to do," he said. "Break
into a man's room this way."

"I'm not armed, Mr. Fargo."

She wore a simple dark dress that reached to the
floor and a scarf that caught her shining hair at the
back. Her eyes gleamed with anxiety but also a hint
of amusement. He decided to pursue the amusement
rather than the anxiety. Put her at her ease. She was
barely out of her teens.

"Let's see now. You're really an Indian here to
scalp me."

She laughed, a girlish giggle. "Not hardly."

"You're a foreign agent and you're going to relieve
me of all my secrets."

This time she only smiled. "I think you know better than that, Mr. Fargo."

He went over to his bureau, poured himself a belt of whiskey, picked up one of three cigarettes he'd rolled himself last night. "One more guess: I'm having a dream. I have to be because I've never seen anybody as beautiful as you while I was awake."

This time the girl blushed. It only enhanced her subtle elegance. "Sister Salvation has warned us that flattery is Satan's most dangerous weapon."

"So you're from Sister Salvation."

"She is the path and the way to heaven."

"And I'll bet she told you that herself."

"Please don't make fun of Sister Salvation. She is enlightened in a way no other human being is. It would be a sin for me to sit here and hear her belittled."

He felt sorry for the girl. Sister Salvation was pretty clearly a con artist.

He lighted his cigarette, exhaled. "Let's be friends, all right? Obviously the Sister sent you here for a reason. Why don't you tell me about it?"

"One of the Guardians saw you this morning with Jane Connolly."

"That's right. She's under the impression that Sister Salvation had her sister, Jenna, murdered."

The girl shuddered. "That's impossible. Sister Salvation is stern sometimes because God tells her to be. But she is stern only to protect sinners from falling deeper into the pit of their sins."

Fargo suppressed a laugh. The girl was so fervent she was reciting Sister Salvation verbatim.

"So she's going to save my soul, is she?"

"You're being sarcastic again. Belittling."

"Well, since I'm still not sure why she sent you here, that's the only thing I can guess she's trying to do. Bring me to salvation."

He took more smoke in; it hung blue in the melancholy light of this late autumn afternoon. "You haven't told me your name."

"Kate Doyle."

"Well, listen, Kate Doyle. What is it you'd like from me?"

"What Sister Salvation would like from you, Mr. Fargo, is for you to go to Jane Connolly to plead with her to call off this rally tonight." Kate settled her slim hands together on her lap. Fargo envied the hell out of that lap. What a nice place it would be to spend some time.

"Now why would I go and do a thing like that?"

"For the sake of the town. There will be great trouble. That's what Sister Salvation fears. She has these visions—of future events."

"I see." Another suppressed laugh. It wouldn't be hard to predict that there'd be trouble at the rally—especially if your own thugs are starting it.

"The sheriff won't stop it because the wealthy people are for it. They're sinners, Mr. Fargo. They are not pure of heart. They want Satan to hold sway in this town."

So young, earnest, foolish. Once again, he felt sad for her. Part of his sadness, though, was the fact that he would never be able to visit his desire upon her. She was old enough, beautiful enough, thrilling enough in her gentle way—but her mind was on some other planet, some realm that was the exclusive property of a con artist named Sister Salvation.

She stood up, moving with a poise and grace that was a pleasing surprise. Sister Salvation might be a grifter but maybe she ran a pretty good finishing school for young girls.

"May I tell Sister that you'll talk to Jane Connolly?"

"Jane's not going to listen to me. I don't want to hurt your feelings here, but nobody should have a hold on a town the way Sister Salvation has a hold on this one."

"But she's doing it for God. And the enlightenment of the people."

He walked over to her and touched her shoulder. "Now you're going to get mad when I say this but listen to me. I've been around people like Sister Salvation before. Somewhere in that fort of hers you're going to find where she keeps all her money. Robbery money."

"You're accusing her of being a thief?" She was ready to get defensive, angry again. Her dark eyes blazed. This pagan was doing the unthinkable—imparting to Sister Salvation the meanest of motives. As if she were a common criminal.

"I'm saying that she's no doubt put aside a lot of money and valuables for herself."

"But the people around here are poor."

"I read in your newspaper this morning about the number of holdups that go on around this territory. And I was told that the good Sister keeps a number of—" He smiled, touched her cheek. "Let's say that she keeps a number of somewhat disreputable gentlemen working for her. Men who'd know how to pull off all these robberies."

She kept her temper but took his hand from her cheek. "From everything I've heard about you, Mr. Fargo, I don't think you have any room to talk when it comes to being disreputable. And as far as some of those, well, rather rough men she hires, you never know when some mob will try to storm the fort. The Sister needs those men to make sure that the fort stays safe. And everybody in it. The Bible says that we have the right to protect ourselves."

"The Bible also warns against false prophets."

Her face turned the violet color of barely contained rage. She pushed past him to the door. Turned as she opened it and said: "You've called her a liar, a thief and now a false prophet. I never want to see you again as long as I live, Mr. Fargo."

Going out, she slammed the door very hard. Almost as hard as Fargo had slammed it coming in.

9

Kate had a difficult time concentrating on the wash that afternoon. She took a wicker basket of it along with the washboard and soap down to the river and proceeded to perform one of her regular duties—keeping everybody in the compound in clean clothes.

Ordinarily, the jays and bluebirds and cardinals that settled on the grass and rocks and trees along her washing site were good companions for her. She spoke to them and she pretended that they spoke back to her. She'd always found solace in nature and in animals, and this kind of proximity to both made her washing chores easy.

But not today.

Fargo's cautionary words had had more of an effect on her than she'd wanted them to. She found herself thinking of all he said and hinted at where Sister Salvation was concerned. Could anybody possibly be as devious as he painted the good Sister? She didn't see how that was possible. She knew she was naïve in many ways but she loved Sister Salvation and trusted her.

She washed the clothes, soaking them in the river and then soaping them and scrubbing them on the washboard. She worked so hard that her lovely hands were raw and red from it. The wind and the birdsong and the sweet scents from the nearby forest were lost on her today.

Skye just couldn't be right. He must have had the Sister confused with somebody else. If he spent even twenty minutes with the Sister he'd be able to see how wrong he was. He'd be able to see that she was indeed God's messenger set here upon the earth. He'd be able to see that a troubled soul like his own could find peace and harmony if only he turned himself and his destiny over to Sister Salvation.

Kate often sang here along the riverbank. She loved religious songs, the ones about heaven especially. She dreamed, both sleeping and awake, of heaven and what she would see and hear and feel when she got there. That was the kind of thing she wished she could convince Skye of.

When the washing was done, she piled everything into the wicker basket and started back toward the fort. She didn't have to go far before she saw the large wagon pulled up to the back gate. She wondered what it was for. Like any place, the fort had its own rumor mill. There was all kinds of speculation about the wagon, but none that really sounded believable to her.

She didn't mind it when people gossiped as long as it didn't get vicious. But a few of the people in the compound had wondered aloud if the Sister wasn't going to take off on them.

They were as cynical as poor Skye Fargo.

Hack Heller was getting some exercise. He was beating up a prisoner. He used fists, feet, even a few head-butts. Sometimes he slapped him. Sometimes he kneed him. Sometimes he spit on him. A feller had to vary his attack of beating somebody half to death; otherwise it could get darned boring.

There had been a series of minor break-ins in town

and Heller wanted to solve them. He wanted folks to know that he wasn't just all brawn. There was one big problem. Heller had no idea who was behind the crimes.

He did have other things running through his mind however. There was this gal, this June Mae Butterworth, and Hack wanted her as he had never wanted any woman in his life. He could barely sleep for thinking of her. Not even servicing himself helped; five minutes later his mind would be fixed on her again.

Now it so happened that June Mae Butterworth was married to Calvin Butterworth, a man who had trouble with the bottle. He'd be all right for three months, everybody in town clapping him on the back and telling him how good it was to see him sober, but then for no apparent reason he'd take up the bottle again. And he'd be so drunk for a week that he'd literally wind up behind some store sleeping it off while June Mae stayed home with the kiddies and prayed all the night through that Calvin wasn't lying dead somewhere. Nobody could ever figure out how a nice gal like June Mae could love and stand by somebody like Calvin. But she sure did.

One night Heller was heading home from a drinking session of his own when he saw Calvin lying facedown in an alley. Heller threw him over his shoulder and carried him home. He wasn't being civic-minded. He wanted a glimpse of June Mae. And he got one.

After dropping Calvin off, Heller got the idea. He spent the next morning crouched in the weeds to the west of the Butterworth shanty. Around noon Calvin stumbled out, no doubt headed to the farm where he worked as a hand, and Heller moved in. He told June Mae that if she wouldn't have sex with him he'd take it out on her husband. But not even that threat worked. She said she could never live with herself afterward. And she said that if Calvin ever found out, he would never be able to touch her in a husbandly way again. . . .

The man Heller was beating up at the moment was none other than Calvin Butterworth.

Heller was hitting the prisoner with right hooks. And having a hell of a good time. He'd never concentrated on right hooks before. They were fun to throw but he would have to soak his hands a long time tonight after a whupping like this one.

The only thing Hack said—and he said it over and over—was "Why don't you just admit you busted into them stores, Calvin? I'll see that the judge goes easy on you. I promise I will."

Heller stopped when Calvin gave up screaming and collapsed into a mess of sweaty, bloody humanity on the floor of the little shed that was out back of the sheriff's office for just such a purpose. It wasn't any fun punching or stomping on an unconscious man. Hearing the man beg, hearing the man sob, hearing the man scream—these were all vital elements of the fun of beating somebody up in the first place.

The wooden shed wasn't much bigger than a cell. Perfect for Heller's purposes.

A knock on the door. He knew who it would be and what she was there for. Hack Heller was a much gratified man. He was gonna get his wish after all.

June Mae Butterworth was out of breath. "I've been looking for him for the past two hours—" She looked past him, to where her husband lay moaning and now out of his head.

Heller said, "I'm just takin' a little break, June Mae. Need to give my knuckles a rest. Then I'll get back to business on him. You and I both know Calvin's been breakin' into those stores."

Her anger was such that she could barely speak. "You know that's a lie, Hack."

Heller smiled. "Of course a man's mind can be

changed, June Mae. A man's mind might forget all about whalin' on a certain feller if a certain lady was to agree to meet him tonight by that big granite boulder down on Owl Creek.''

And that was how Hack Heller came to have carnal knowledge of June Mae Butterworth on the night of October 17, right out there in the moonlight just after suppertime. He would ordinarily have scheduled the tryst for later in the evening. But this was the night he was to make off with Sister Salvation's robbery loot. June Mae and all that cash in the same evening— he'd have to mark this night down on a calendar somewhere.

10

Jenna had been the religious one. So now as Jane Connolly knelt at the Communion rail in the church, she found herself unable to concentrate on praying. She wasn't even quite sure she believed in any kind of afterlife. Every other form of life died, why shouldn't the human being? And why would the human being have a soul when none of the other creatures would?

Her doubts had cost her a marriage. Her fiancé broke it off when she told him that she wasn't going to convert to his religion and would not, herself, attend church in the religion she'd been raised in. Breaking off the marriage had turned out to be all right, anyway. Through all their arguments she found that he was really more concerned with the perception of going to church than with church itself. He was a businessman and worried about how it would look if he and his family didn't trek to services every Sunday.

But, probably just for tonight, Jane found that kneeling here in the early shadows of evening, the votive lights the only illumination, the faded scent of incense on the air and an especially lovely statue of the Virgin looking down upon her . . . she found that she felt close to Jenna.

Such a jumble of thoughts and memories. Tearing up one moment, smiling the next. She hoped she could keep herself under control tonight at the rally. She wanted her speech to be strong. She didn't want it weepy and self-pitying. Even without the murder of her sister, there were innumerable good reasons to finally rid this town of Sister Salvation.

If there *was* a rally.

Once again she had thoughts of standing on the bench, waiting anxiously for the crowd—and nobody showing up. Or maybe only Sister Salvation's gunnies would show up. Maybe they'd encircle the park bench and people would see them and be frightened off. The gunnies only rarely came to town but they were such a fierce looking bunch that they generally caused people to flee to their homes. Nobody wanted to tangle with them.

"Excuse me."

The voice jarred Jane from her thoughts. She looked up to see Father McGuire standing behind her. The chunky, bald, middle-aged priest said, "I just wanted to give you my personal condolences, Jane. The folks at the mortuary told me that you wanted her buried in the churchyard here. I've taken care of all that."

"Thank you, Father."

She stood up.

"I've also said prayers for you, Jane. For tonight. The rally."

She smiled. "I'll need them. Maybe nobody'll show up."

"Oh, I doubt that. I think Sister Salvation has about run her course here. I sense that everywhere I go. I think people have finally had enough."

"She killed my sister."

"That's the assumption. But—and I hope this doesn't upset you—it seems a strange thing for her to do. She had to know she'd be the first one to get blamed."

"That's what several people have told me, Father. But I just can't think of why anybody else would want to kill her."

She saw him avert his eyes momentarily. The dancing light from the bank of candles played across his face. He'd obviously wanted to say something and then had checked himself.

"You were going to say something, Father?"

"No, that's fine."

"Now you have to say it. Otherwise I'll start wondering what you were holding back."

"I just—well, you knew all about her relationship with Evan Chandler."

"She broke it off."

"That's my point, Jane. She broke it off and from what I understand, he was very angry and hurt."

"You're saying he killed her?"

"I'm just saying other people had motives, too. I'm not saying anybody in particular."

"I can't believe you're defending Sister Salvation."

"Jane—listen to me. I'm not defending or accusing anybody. I personally think Sister Salvation is a sham."

"Then why defend her?"

He sighed. "Jane, all I'm saying is that I don't want some lynch mob going to the old fort and dragging her up to some tree. And that's the mood this town is in right now."

"Well, if you're right that she's about run her course here—maybe this rally will give her the final nudge. If we get enough people to show up—enough people to show her we aren't afraid of her—maybe she'll decide to leave on her own. That way you don't have to worry about lynching or anything else. If she didn't kill my sister. But if there's evidence against her—"

He took her hand. "Then I think we're in agreement.

All I want is for everything to be fair. We need law and order restored here, Jane. And we'll never have that if we start convicting people with nothing to go on." Then he smiled as he took his hand away. "I think this is only the second time I've ever seen you in church. I've talked to you plenty of times on the street. But never here."

"I know. Jenna would get a good laugh out of this. She'd probably say it was worth dying just to get me to come to church."

"She was a very good woman, your sister."

"Yes, she was."

"I counted her as a real friend."

"The feeling was mutual, Father, believe me."

He smiled. "Thanks for telling me that. Makes me feel better."

Now it was her turn to touch *his* arm. "I'm not going to lead a lynch mob tonight, Father. You don't have to worry about that. I just want to clear the air. And make it unmistakable to Sister Salvation that we don't want her around here anymore."

"You're going to inspire a lot of people tonight, Jane. You're a born speaker."

"I'll just keep thinking of Jenna, Father. That's what's going to get me through all this." Tears broke her voice. "I loved her so much, Father. She was the best friend I ever had."

The priest left her alone. She sat in the front pew thinking about her sister. The rally wouldn't start for another ninety minutes yet.

The man in black reached the center of town just after the supper hour. Said hi to most folks and most folks said hi right back and then they all went their separate ways.

Earlier in the day, he had stashed a rifle in a special place and had now come to claim it. Or would soon, anyway. There really wasn't a rush. The rally was an hour off.

The thing he wanted to check out was the alley. You lived or died in that alley. You had to get in, do the deed, and get out before folks could figure out what was going on. There would be a moment of panic—of hysteria—and the killer would use that moment to escape.

The night was damp now. Chilly. The saloons were still open, so everything in the vicinity was noisy with coarse laughter and shouts.

The street was clear. Nobody watching. Nobody he could see, anyway. Of course, he might have overlooked somebody. A pair of eyes in a window behind a curtain. But the risk was worth taking. Well worth it.

The lamplight from the street carried over to the alley in a faint, muzzy way. The stench of the latrine twenty yards away on the grass was so strong it brought tears to his eyes. The stuff they used to keep the smell down was as bad as the smell itself.

He checked for drunks. Drunks liked alleys. They crapped in them, peed in them, ate in them, slept in them. Once in a while through the fog of their alcoholic delirium they'd wake up for a minute or two and see things. Odd things. Things they'd remember, though. Most of the time it wasn't important, what they remembered. But the killer didn't want any drunks around when the time came.

The alley was drunk-free.

The next thing to check was the stack of boxes that had been conveniently left in back of the store he planned to use. Wooden crates, really. Eminently stackable. Weighed nothing. And tall enough, stacked, to put him right on the roof.

A stray dog came along. A male mongrel with an almost idiotically sweet face. Kind of stupid looking, actually, but endearing.

The man in black bent over and petted it. The dog licked the killer's hand and he smiled. There was a lot to smile about, the way everything was taking shape.

There wouldn't be any problems tonight.

Not a single one as far as he could see; not a single, solitary one.

The rally was scheduled to start soon. Jane Connolly stood next to the park bench she planned to stand on, nervously twisting her hands. She wasn't egotistical about tonight. She didn't care if she was humiliated by only a few people showing up. What depressed her was the thought that the town wasn't ready to stand up to Sister Salvation.

The ten-year-old Jenkins boy, a pudgy, towheaded kid, came up to her. "My mom and dad was havin' an argument about you at supper, Miss Connolly," he said.

She was thankful for the distraction. Talking to a ten-year-old was better than just standing here stewing. "Oh? Why were they arguing about me?"

"Dad said that nobody was a-gonna show up here tonight."

"I see."

"But Mom—she said there'll be a lot of people." He looked at the empty street. The saloons were going full blast at the far end of the block but that was the only excitement unless you considered watching a bored horse tied to a hitching post drop road apples exciting.

Jane smiled. "So what do you think?"

He shrugged. She could see that he was enamored of her. She had the kind of sweet, unthreatening looks of a schoolmarm. She was the sort of woman little boys always developed crushes on. "Well, I hope Mom's right. For your sake. But like my dad said, a lot of people are mighty scared of Sister Salvation. He said that when our neighbor Mr. Doakes spoke up agin her, two nights later somebody shot his two horses."

"That's why we have to fight her. We can't let her get away with things like that."

He nodded. Gulped. His eyes beamed with innocent adoration. "You sure look nice tonight, Miss Connolly."

"Well, thank you."

"Well, I guess I'd better git."

"I appreciate you stopping by."

"You do?" He sounded excited. He had one more dream to tuck under his pillow tonight. He grinned and ran off.

Funny how little moments like that could make you feel better. In some ways she felt foolish for making so much of it. But talking to the boy had made her feel part of the community again, reminded her that there were some awfully decent people here. Reminded her that there was a very good reason that they were all so afraid of Sister Salvation. Killing two horses like that in the middle of the night. That kind of terrorism was the best way to keep a town cowed.

"Good evening, Jane."

She turned to see Mrs. William Redfearn no less walking down the street toward her. Mrs. Redfearn's husband was one of the most powerful men in the area. "I see the crowd hasn't started arriving yet, dear. But don't worry. All my friends said they're coming—with or without their husbands." She was a large woman given to dark silk dresses and large flowery hats even in the autumn. "It's funny, isn't it? The women are more willing to stand up to Sister Salvation than the men. My husband is under the impression that the Sister will pay everybody back who shows up for the rally tonight." She laughed. "I told him he was a cowering old fool and to not expect me too early. I said I just might grab some of the gals and have a liquor party at the hotel." She winked. "You should've seen his face. He thought I was serious."

Then, making Mrs. Redfearn's prediction come true, a surrey and a wagon came into view at the north end of the long street. On the wagon seat sat three women; four more stood in the wagon bed.

Mrs. Redfearn said, "Looks like the rally is finally ready to start."

This is for you, Jenna, Jane thought. *Dear sister, this is for you.*

The Trailsman ate supper in the café half a block from his hotel. The place was more crowded than he'd seen it.

There was an anxiety you could feel but also an excitement. Though most people wouldn't admit it, they liked to see a limited amount of trouble. Maybe they didn't want to see anybody get killed but they wouldn't mind seeing somebody wounded.

Grandpas with Old Testament beards; fierce, hard, middle-aged farmers; weary-looking farm wives; kids who kept glancing out the front window to see if a crowd was forming yet. It wasn't and it made Fargo think that it would be funny if the only people who showed up were the crowd watchers and not the crowd at all.

Fargo looked out the window, too. He was keeping an eye out for gunnies. The only ones he knew of were Sister Salvation's and if they showed up, that would mean trouble for sure. It was unlikely that they would let Jane stand up there and denounce their boss lady without some kind of retaliation. They might not believe in the good Sister's divinity but they sure enough believed in the cover she'd given them while they robbed various and sundry places.

Somebody in the back of the café started playing an accordion. It was such a festive sound that the tension level dropped immediately. Hard to stay dour and apprehensive when your feet wanted to tap out a rhythm.

A couple of little towheaded kids maybe five and six—obviously brother and sister—stood in the aisle between the tables and performed a dance more notable for its enthusiasm than its skill. Blond hair flying, huge grins splitting their faces, they only added to the suddenly changed and happy atmosphere.

Fargo was just finishing up his second cup of coffee when he sensed somebody approaching, looked up and saw Hack Heller standing there.

Heller didn't ask if he could sit down. He just sat.

"You tell that friend of yours I don't want any trouble tonight. I don't want nobody talkin' about goin' out to the fort and raisin' any kind of hell."

The best way to deal with a bully was to stay low-key. Pretty soon he'd start trying to figure out how you could stay so calm in the face of his wrath. You were supposed to be afraid of him, right? Where was that quiver in the Trailsman's voice, anyway?

Fargo said calmly, "That come from the town council, did it?"

"It comes from me, Fargo. I'm the law here, not the town council."

"Gosh, and here I thought I saw a sheriff's badge on Dave Sadler."

"You know what a load of bull that is. They keep him on just to save face. He might've been somebody special once but he ain't any longer."

Fargo leaned back in his chair and rolled himself a cigarette. "I'm hearing a lot of stories about the Sister."

"Yeah? Like what?"

"Like how her gunnies have been robbing a lot of stagecoaches and banks since they got here."

"So what? Who hasn't heard that one?"

Fargo said, "She probably has a lot of money out there. Stashed away, I mean."

"She probably spent it all." Heller was trying to sound calm but it wasn't working. His agitation over Fargo's remark could probably be felt clear across the dining room.

"Maybe, maybe not. If it's still out there, that'll be a considerable amount of loot."

"Well, you don't worry about that, Fargo. All you worry about is makin' sure that Connolly girl don't stir up a mob and lead 'em out there."

"That won't happen, Heller. She just wants Sister Salvation to leave. She doesn't want her to die."

Heller stood up. "She don't want to cross me, Fargo. Remind her that I run this town."

Fargo smiled. "The way you swagger around, Heller, that's kind of hard to forget."

Heller gave him a cold look and swaggered away.

Dave Sadler found himself at his wife's grave, at the top of a bluff lit by the half moon and chilled by a harsh wind. You go through life thinking that you'll die before your spouse and then one day she just isn't there any more. Didn't make any sense. He was a brooder and his wife had been a woman who loved and enjoyed almost every day of her life. You'd think that God or fate or destiny or whatever ran the world would take that into account. Sadler didn't care all that much for life and here he was the one who lived on.

She wouldn't have noticed, for instance, the disrepair the graveyard had fallen into. She would've just knelt down before the grave of the friend she'd come to visit and said her prayers and filled herself with the warmth and radiance of pleasant memories.

She wouldn't have noticed all the dog turds that

hadn't been raked up from the grass that needed mowing; the dirty words that had been cut into the gravestones with knives or nails; the section of fence that drooped; the lightning-cracked branches that had been left to rot instead of being hauled away.

But Dave Sadler noticed them and they churned his stomach and soured his soul. He'd gone to the town council innumerable times about the graveyard. They made promises and promises and promises but nothing was ever done. But hell, if it bothered him so much, why didn't he round up a bunch of civic-minded citizens and take on the job himself?

A good sound reason was why. Because right after his wife died, he was so far down he was in no way prepared for the arrival of Sister Salvation, a woman who damn near stole the town away. Gladville had always lived with vice, and kept a tight check on it. Yes, there was violence, but no more than what you'd find in any other frontier town.

But it was as if half the town had been waiting for a messiah of some kind. And that was the Sister herself.

The religious folks took away his authority. They didn't break the law in any way he could prove. He sank under the humiliation of the Sister and the gloom over his wife's death. He got older than his years. The deterioration of the graveyard was only one of the things he didn't pay active attention to.

Now, he said, "I'm glad you're not here to see this. You'd be just as ashamed of me as I am of myself."

The wind whipped the words from the mouth of the lone figure silhouetted against the night sky, forlorn and beaten, unaware of the fall leaves ripping from their branches and slapping across his face.

It was as if he was a stranger to himself, somebody who resembled Dave Sadler but was not Dave Sadler.

He said to his wife, his voice shaking, "Tell me what to do, honey. You always told me before. Please tell me what to do now."

Fargo stood under the overhang of his hotel, watching the empty street begin to fill up with riders, wagons and townspeople coming in clutches, gaggles and gangs. The people didn't seem angry or gloomy at all. They were more like a crowd going to a political rally than a crowd headed to hear a denunciation of a suspect religious leader.

Shawls, bonnets, even a few ear-flapped hats lent the impression that it was colder than it actually was. From his vantage point, Fargo was able to see Jane Connolly standing on her park bench. She was smiling. She obviously figured that people responded better to smiles than to scowls, even when the business was serious.

A traveling salesman—his clothes and his manner making his occupation clear came out and stood on the porch with him. "Name's Amherst. Charlie Amherst."

Fargo nodded. He wasn't much for small talk and he sensed a whole pile of it ready to be laid at his feet.

"Quite a crowd." Amherst pressed some wrinkles out of his checkered suit jacket with the palms of his beefy hands.

"Going to be nice-sized."

"I remember this town in the old days. Wide open. But that sheriff—forget his name—"

"Sadler."

"Right. Sadler. He kept a tight rein on things. There was a lot of violence before he came but he clamped down hard. But the town was still a lot of fun."

"Maybe it'll be like that again."

"Sure hope so. Damned saloons might as well close up right after supper. That's a hell of a thing for a man like me. Gets real boring sittin' in your room and smokin' cigars and wishin' there was somethin' to do."

"Yeah, I'll bet."

Amherst looked around. "That damn chili I ate gave me gas. Think I'll go for a little walk. Looks like I'll have to take the alley, the street's so crowded."

He doffed his derby and set off.

Fargo rolled a smoke. The crowd exceeded anything he'd expected. He was on the look-see for Sister Salvation's gunnies. Men like that tended to be pretty easily identifiable. There were exceptions but not many.

There was a bit of trouble with a spooked horse, and a drunk got sick and vomited all over a respectable lady. Then a three-year-old got isolated from his folks and wailed with hair-curling terror until he was reunited.

Somebody in the front of the crowd had a pitch pipe and started the crowd singing a familiar hymn. It was about midway through the song before everybody, including all the men who thought that singing was somehow effete, joined in.

With everybody singing, it was sort of stirring. These were, like Fargo himself, common folk who worked hard and stayed to acting within the law and tried to keep their surroundings civil and beneficial to as many people as possible. These were the people who were building the West. Even Fargo started to sing along.

When the song was finished, Jane Connolly addressed the crowd.

"I sure wasn't expecting this many people. I can't tell you what this means to me—and to the memory of my sister. If she had to die, I'm glad it at least spurred all of you to come out and support our cause.

"And you know what that cause is. Most of you folks are churchgoers. But you don't butt into other people's business and you don't try to tell other people how to live. That's how religion should be handled. It's a part of everyday life but to each his own—you have the right to believe or not believe, and to follow your belief as long as it doesn't intrude on anybody else's life.

"I don't have to tell you that that's all changed since Sister Salvation came to town and started trying to run our lives for us."

That line brought the night's first burst of applause.

The man in black waited until the crowd was watching Jane Connolly before easing away and heading back toward the alley. A few drunks came in and out of the saloons as he walked back up the street but they paid no attention. Like everybody else, they watched the slight, fetching figure of Jane Connolly on the park bench, addressing the rally.

He walked a block farther than was necessary. If anybody happened to be watching, they would see nothing more memorable than somebody passing into the night. No association whatsoever with what was about to happen.

He waited until even the lamplight failed to illumine the night before starting down the alley toward the back of the store and the hidden rifle.

Deep breaths. Needed to steady the nerves. Odd how easy things always were when you were planning them, but when you actually got to the place and the moment, you began seeing all the pitfalls that could expose you. And you had to confront your own fear as well. Taking a life wouldn't be that difficult. But being caught and paying for taking that life was another matter entirely.

The crowd was getting warmed up now. Every few minutes it went into a kind of war-whoop mode, yelling, whistling and applauding. Delicate Jane Connolly probably didn't think of herself as a rabble-rouser but that's just what she was. And just what she was doing.

The word had been that Sister Salvation's gunnies might be down here tonight. If they were, the man in black felt sorry for them. The mood this crowd was getting in, the gunnies would be lucky if the crowd didn't run them down and crush them underfoot. No matter how many guns they had, a handful of gunnies were useless against an angry mob. Especially a mob that had been accumulating rage for as long as this one had been.

The man in black kept surveying the alley that stretched before him. The only traffic back here was a tomcat who padded around looking for either food or entertainment. The tom looked awfully bored in the way only a cat can looked bored. Total monotony.

He was starting to feel confident again. This was all going to go off without a hitch. Not even the escape would be difficult. Not with the horse he had ground-tied in the field out back of the store whose roof he would fire from. The firearm would be gone and so would its user. No evidence left behind by the time somebody from the crowd rushed back here to try to find the shooter.

There was always that long, frozen moment following an assassination when everybody in the crowd—even the lawmen who were paid to respond instantly—didn't know what to do. Panic was the operative word. Panic and even a bit of disbelief. That person who'd been speaking just a moment ago, now riddled with bullets and lying on the ground? How could something like that have happened?

Then a few people in the crowd would swing into action. And it was at that point that the shooter needed to be long gone.

He came abreast of the boxes. Time to stack them. Time to climb them. Time to take care of Jane Connolly.

*　　*　　*

Charlie Amherst, the salesman Fargo had been talking to on the front porch of the hotel a few minutes earlier, felt his gas attack begin to wane. Good. Maybe he'd try to scout up a gal for the evening. Hated to go to a crib and spend all night farting. One thing Charlie did by God was treat everybody equal—except of course for Lutherans, Mexicans, fat women, doctors who scorned the patent medicines he sold, and people who had different-colored eyes—and prostitutes were included among that list. You wouldn't visit somebody's home when you were having a gas attack, would you? Sit in the parlor and fart into their nice new chairs?

Well, why would you treat cathouses any differently? He didn't want to be up in bed all night with some amply endowed farm girl and have to keep apologizing for passing gas. He had a lot more respect for them than that. And for himself.

But the walking was taking care of the gas. He was back to dreaming of an hour in a room with a gal who just yearned to make him happy in any way he cared to be *made* happy. His wife, God love her—she was the mother of his three children, after all, and as such he had both respect and admiration for her—just didn't understand about how a man wanted more than a woman who lay submissively beneath him, enduring it more than enjoying it. And completely unwilling to experiment. That was the nice thing about farm gals. You could poke, prod, pillory them any way you wanted, as long as you didn't slap them around—that cost extra—and they'd at least *pretend* that they liked it.

The alley. Charlie hated latrines but his bladder wasn't what it used to be. What he usually did was find the latrine and then find a nearby place to urinate. That way if anybody complained that he wasn't

67

using the latrine itself, he could just say that he'd gotten confused and that this section of the grass sure looked like the latrine to him. Luckily, this wasn't one of those places where they had signs marking off the latrine area. Hard to pretend he didn't see them.

Charlie found the latrine, walked a good distance from the assaultive hole that had been dug—holding his breath all the time because of the god-awful stench—and proceeded to unbutton his trousers.

He was whizzing away when he became aware—through some sixth sense—that something was going on behind his back. Not the rally, he'd been well aware of that. Hard not to be what with all the enthusiastic noises it made. No, this was something else.

He finished his business and turned around and saw it.

A figure in black. Stacking boxes behind a store. And suddenly the figure was climbing those boxes and jumping onto the roof.

Now Charlie Amherst was many things, but stupid wasn't one of them. You see a guy stacking boxes that he obviously means to use as a ladder of some kind and all sorts of dark suspicions come to mind. Charlie couldn't think of a single good reason why somebody would be doing this.

Charlie was about to go over and take a second look when the rifle appeared, glinting in the wan moonlight.

Not too hard to put this whole thing together. Crates as a ladder leading to a roof.

A roof as a place to shoot from. And now a rifle.

What you were talking here was an assassination.

Charlie himself didn't want to get shot, which he most certainly would if he tried to stop the shooter. All the killer would have to do was turn around and open fire on Charlie. And then whip back and shoot the target he'd come to shoot.

What Charlie needed to do was find some law, and fast.

That was when he turned and started to run, and tripped into three empty barrels.

The man in black might not have heard Charlie stumble into the barrels if there hadn't been a pause in Jane Connolly's speech.

But there was that silence and Charlie did trip into the barrels and the killer did happen to hear him.

He ran to the back edge of the roof.

At first it was difficult to see anything but some overweight tomcat wandering down the alley. But his eyes soon adjusted to the deep shadows along the backs of the stores. And there was Charlie, sprawled face-down on the ground, the barrels all around him.

At any other time, the sight might have been comic. A chubby man in a cheap salesman's suit with his derby lying on the ground next to him. It was like something you saw in a traveling comedy show.

Two important questions immediately came to mind. First, what exactly had the chubby man seen? Had he tripped because he was drunk or had he tripped because he was hurrying to get help after seeing somebody on the roof with a rifle? Second, why wasn't the chubby man moving? The first thing a man in his situation would do is pick himself up. But he was still lying there amidst the barrels. Why?

Too risky to just let this situation alone. Something needed to be done about it. And right now. If the chubby man had actually seen a rifle, then what he'd been trying to do was find a lawman to stop the assassination.

He had no choice. Back down the crates to the alley floor. Walking carefully over to the chubby man. And just in time, as things played out, because the chubby man was just now—and quite groggily—starting to revive.

Still unaware of the man in black, Charlie put his hands on the center of one of the barrels he'd tipped over and pushed himself shakily to his feet. He stood upright but he gave the impression he might not be doing so for long. His legs trembled, looking as if they might not support him.

Then he turned and saw the killer. And the killer saw why it had taken him so long to rouse himself. A long bloody gash was clear to see on the right side of the chubby man's forehead. He must have knocked himself out.

What happened next happened silently, against the overwhelming noise of the rally at its highest peak—responding to Jane Connolly's urge to put the community back together again rather than leave it divided the way it was now, to make sure that neither the town council nor the sheriff's department was intimidated in any way by Sister Salvation.

A perfect time for a pair of shots to be smothered by crowd noise. A perfect time for a killer to claim his victim.

The chubby man turned his head only once. He saw that he could neither protect himself nor escape in time before the inevitable happened. In huge, pathetic pantomime he splayed his hands over his face, entreaty in his sad-hound eyes.

Two shots. Clean, on-target. Two shots. Each lost in the noise of the rally.

No time to drag the corpse out of the way. No time to make sure the chubby man was dead. Had to assume that two shots in the chest had made him so. At the least, he wasn't going to get up and run for help.

Now back to the crates and the roof and the reason the killer was here in the first place. But now there was a certain panic in the killer's movements. The rhythm had been broken; the concentration. He needed to bring all his attention to bear on the rifle and then on the target.

Belly-crawling up to the edge of the roof. Had at first planned to stand up. Too risky. Lying flat like this would slow down the escape time. But it had to be done.

Concentrate. Entire mind focused on the victim. That pretty face now so earnest as she continued to stir the crowd. That damned irritating bass drum booming every couple minutes. The crowd cheering again. Jane Connolly waving the papers she was reading from.

Taking aim. Steady. Focus. The forehead. Good, clean shot. Two shots, just in case. Up high enough so that even if the crowd surged closer to her, none of them would be hurt.

Plenty of time. No need to be nervous. No need to be scared. Clean shots followed by a clean getaway.

Same spot on the forehead.

Steady now. Ready now.

The rally was rolling in earnest.

"She came among us pretending to be our friend. 'The Lord's Messenger,' she called herself. And at first that's what she seemed to be. She spoke a gospel of love and kindness and tolerance. But eventually that gospel changed. Most folks didn't know it at first.

"But she started to ask us to look around. Not so that we could help our neighbors. Or see if there was any way we could help them as Christ would have helped them. No, she began asking us to find fault. To begin to suspect the worst of our friends and neighbors. And to start sending them little notes. Unsigned, of course. Start telling them that they weren't living by the one true word—by Sister Salvation's word.

"Think back to how our town used to be. Not per-

71

fect, I'm not saying that. Too wild for its own good. That's the best way to say it. Too many scarlet women, too much gambling, too much violence and saloons that took every penny a workingman had. We needed a remedy. Nobody would deny that.

"But is this the remedy? Turning neighbor against neighbor? Giving all your hard-earned money to a woman who wishes to live in secret, a woman we rarely see any more? A woman who has cowed our sheriff. A woman who has created 'Guardians' to write down everything they see and hear in our streets.

"There are cases where children have started taunting their parents for being sinners. One boy even began beating his father with a broom when he found his parents making love. He said that Sister Salvation had said that all intercourse was sinful unless the object was to have children. She has even used children as 'Guardians' at the town school so they can report on other children.

"And what about all the violence that comes down on people she considers sinners? Many of you here tonight were written up by Guardians and found your windows smashed, or your wagon burned to the ground, or some member of your family mysteriously beaten.

"I don't think we have to ask ourselves who's behind all these crimes, do we? Even if the sheriff pretends not to know, we know otherwise. We know that it's Sister Salvation's thugs who come after us in the dead of night, who scare our children and report on us back to the fortress up there on the hill.

"She's probably watching us right now. I'm told she takes field glasses and stands in the turret and watches us. As if she's a grand queen and we're nothing more than peasants.

"Well, I say it's time we took back our town. We need a new town council, we need a new sheriff and we need Sister Salvation put in prison or at least run out of town! And I mean in the next twenty-four hours!''

When Jane Connolly finished speaking, the crowd signaled its approval with an explosive round of applause. It looked like a rally where everybody was drunk. The big drum started pounding again. Several men hoisted Jane onto their shoulders and began carrying her down the street. Tent-revival songs were sung. And even the men in the saloons staggered and swaggered their way out to stand on the porches and see what was going on. Torch flames flapped in the wind.

Fargo stood on the boardwalk and watched the marchers stamp past. There was true jubilation in the air. Even the Guardians took on a mantle of silly festiveness as they scribbled down the names of the participants as quickly as they could. If they wrote much faster, they'd break their fingers.

There was little doubt that the rally had been successful and that the majority of the town had found their dignity and voice again and would soon move against Sister Salvation. Humble as it all was, it was like witnessing an important new idea not only being born but being implemented as well.

He finally saw where the marchers were headed and it made sense. They were gathering in front of the nearby sheriff's office. Now it would be Sadler's turn to join in on this new movement, to recover his dignity and purpose as a lawman. If he helped—even better, led—the charge against Sister Salvation, a lot of his past cowardice would be not only forgiven but eventually forgotten. He would regain some of his old reputation as a top lawman.

The torches flamed with a certain grandeur in the wind off the Nebraska prairie. The revival songs had an equally grand beauty. Common, everyday folks singing of a better life out on here on the flattest land God had ever created—land that seemed to go on not just for hours but for centuries. But it would be good land if the town was once again righted, so that its citizens could live in reasonable harmony and not be manipulated by Sister Salvation. There was real joy now in the voices and on the faces of the crowd.

The man in black felt betrayed. And that was sort of funny, when you thought about it. It was as if he had assumed some kind of strange pact with Jane Connolly.

The plan was, Jane, in case you didn't know it, for you to stand on that park bench and for me to shoot you twice in the forehead.

Now what am I supposed to do with you gallivanting off on the shoulders of some men who are carrying you to the sheriff's office? I open fire and I might hit two or three innocent people. They're so close together, a bullet could go through a couple of them.

Now my whole plan has to change.

Thanks a lot, Jane.

Range had to be calculated, and quickly. Could she be killed from here? He would have to take the back of her head instead of the front. And he would have to wait until the crowd gave her some room.

Sick stomach. Pounding headache. Trembling hands. Icy sweat.

It wasn't supposed to have been like this. It was supposed to have been easy.

For the next few minutes, the crowd stayed tight around her as the chant went up to force somebody from the sheriff's office to come out and talk to them. The drum resumed its imposing booming. The torches were hoisted high into the air. An up-tempo religious song was sung, with people clapping along.

All the man with the gun needed was a small wedge

of time when Jane Connolly wasn't surrounded by her admirers, when she wasn't being jostled about.

The back of the head would be fine, he had decided, already envisioning the explosion of hair, flesh, brain matter and bone.

Just two quick shots.

Thirty, forty seconds at most.

And then—

Jane Connolly stepped up on the sidewalk fronting the sheriff's office. She now stood a couple feet above the crowd.

No time to waste.

It had all come down to this moment.

The killer squeezed off two quick shots and then raced to the edge of the roof. Getting off the roof was no problem but when he landed on the ground, a broken bottle was there to rip into the flesh just above the ankle.

The pain was sharp but there was no time to worry about it. No time at all.

====== 11 ======

Fargo was able to judge where the shots came from. While the crowd was in a frenzied mass of people screaming, shouting, pointing to the roof, he pushed, shoved and butted his way up the street. The doc had been standing near Jane while she stormed the sheriff's office; he would take care of her. All Fargo cared about now was getting the shooter.

The four minutes it took him to reach the alley were costly in terms of the shooter's escape. The moment Fargo turned into the alley, he saw two things: the apparently dead body of the salesman he'd just been talking to, and a rider already distant and riding hard in a northerly direction. The shooter had planned his escape as well as he'd planned the assassination itself.

Fargo ran to the livery. Rawlings, the groom, was brushing down a sorrel.

"I need the fastest animal you've got here."

"Your own horse shouldn't be run yet."

"I know. Whatever else you've got, I'll take. And fast."

Rawlings moved with surprising speed and agility for a man his age. He saddled a beautiful palomino. As he got the animal ready, he said, "Belongs to the man owns this place. I don't reckon he'll mind if you use him to catch that shooter. Miss Jane gonna be all right?"

"I don't know yet. But she took two shots. That can't be good."

Fargo was urging the horse into full action even before they had quite cleared the rear of the livery. Within a few minutes all the commotion in the town was behind him and there was just the Nebraska prairie night.

Fargo had time to think through Jane's shooting. He couldn't believe that Sister Salvation would risk her relatively safe perch in this town to kill off a minor political enemy. Determined as Jane was to get rid of her, the Sister still controlled a good share of the town and its citizens. From everything he'd heard about the woman, it would be surprising if she'd get spooked by the two Connolly women and turn killer. Intimidation was her style, not killing.

No sight of the rider. When he bore northeast, Fargo started running the horse along the bank of a wide stream. About a mile up the stream, he saw the black horse the shooter had been riding. It stood head bowed, idly drinking from the water glistening in the moonlight.

Fargo, being a cautious man, assumed this was some kind of clumsy trap. He'd sneak up there and then the killer would open fire from a hiding place.

Smells of water, autumn smoke, leaves crisped by sunlight. Sounds of the stream shooting fast over rocks, a coyote somewhere nearby, and the sound of his own saddle creaking as he eased off the palomino and dropped to the ground.

He was a good twenty yards from the horse. He wondered where the shooter was. There were no good hiding places around here. Except—

He started scanning the trees. Even without all the leaves, the pines and junipers were bunched close enough together that a man could climb up into them and fade away into the darkness. You wouldn't see him until you got right up to the trees.

No shots. No sudden rustling in the pines and junipers. No rifle glint in the moonlight. The shooter's horse still indulging itself in the stream after its long escape run from town.

Damn strange.

He cautiously approached the stream, head moving side to side, finger tense on the trigger of his Colt.

Damn strange indeed.

For the next few minutes, he walked up and down the bank examining footprints. There were six fresh ones and they led right into the water.

There was only one thing to do: Fargo waded in. The stream was maybe three feet deep. He crossed it, holding his Colt above his head as he moved.

He picked up the footsteps on the other side of the stream. They led into timber. A rutted wagon trail angled southward. The footsteps ended at another trail—more of a path, really—that led directly into the shadowy forest that was suddenly alive with the night babblings of various creatures. They were probably amused to see this giant. Entertainment; something new to watch and comment on during the long night.

There was no way he could track the killer through the forest. There just wasn't sufficient light.

The getaway plan was simple but effective. Fargo could pretty much plot the whole thing from scratch. The first thing would be to steal a horse so that when they found it they couldn't tell who'd ridden it. The second thing would be to run the horse hard after you'd shot your target and then leave it along a stream to confuse anybody who might have come after you. And the third thing was to lose yourself in the timber on the other side of the water. Not even an Indian could track you in deep woods at this time of night.

Satisfied that this was the case, Fargo waded back across the stream to his own horse. He rode over to the stolen horse and took the reins. When he got back to town, he wanted to look up the rightful owner. Maybe that person would know something helpful. It was unlikely that the true owner of the animal had had anything to do with the shooting.

Hack Heller hadn't planned on anybody giving him an assist tonight but he was grateful for it, anyway. With a good share of the townspeople standing vigil outside the doc's house, waiting to see if Jane Connolly was going to make it, nobody noticed that Heller wasn't doing his duty. Instead of looking into the killing, he slipped out of town, leaving Dave Sadler to calm people down and start asking folks if they'd seen or heard anything that could help him figure out who'd done the shooting.

Heller headed straight for Sister Salvation's fort. He needed only one man to help him with this operation—a man named Decker who would sneak him into the fort.

Heller rode to his usual lookout post on the hill above the fort. He took his field glasses from his saddlebag and began his survey of the activities below.

They went to bed early, following a communal singing of hymns, and some highfalutin holy talk from Sister Salvation. She was apparently of the mind that the more you slept, the less trouble you could get into, so the fort was generally dark after eight o'clock in the evening.

It had darkened down for the night. A hymn concluded. Sister Salvation urged her flock to be pure in thought and deed—all the usual bullshit you got from religious folk who wanted to pick your pocket—and then the various lanterns strung around the fort started going out.

There was a back gate, and it was here that he was supposed to meet Decker. They had gone over everything twice in the past forty-eight hours. It was simple enough if everything went right. If it didn't go right, there were going to be an awful lot of dead people and Hack Heller didn't plan on being one of them.

The crowd hadn't diminished any.

Fargo worked his way to the front door, knocked. Sheriff Dave Sadler opened the door seconds later. He stood back so Fargo could come in. Then he went out on the small porch and addressed the crowd. "I'm not going to get your hopes up. One of the bullets—for some reason the doc can't explain—bounced off her skull. The other one went in just about her right ear. That's the one that did all the damage."

The people's faces were lighted by the torches they still carried. Expressions of concern alternated with expressions of anger.

A farmer asked, "We seen Fargo go in there. Did he find out anything when he went after the shooter?"

Fargo stepped out on the porch. "I'm pretty sure he stole the horse he was riding. He left it at a stream and then disappeared into the woods on the other side."

"I had a horse stolen last night," said an elderly woman. "I told the sheriff about it this morning."

"That's right," Sadler said to Fargo.

"What'd the horse look like, ma'am?"

She told him. It was definitely the horse that had been drinking from the stream.

"Should we get a posse up?" a man said.

Sadler looked to Fargo.

"I'd wait until tomorrow," Fargo said. "I don't think we could accomplish much tonight."

"If there's any news from inside, I'll come out and

tell you," Sadler said. "But most of you have jobs and such in the morning. You might as well go on home. This could be a long night."

"I feel like goin' right out to that fort and runnin' the Sister clear the hell out of this whole territory," said a young man.

There was a rumble of agreement.

"We don't know that she had anything to do with this," Sadler said. "We don't want to make things worse than they already are. I'll be going out there tonight. I'll be asking her all the questions you want asked. No need for you to worry about it."

"If she had anything to do with it," a swarthy man said. "I say we run every one of 'em off and outlaw the whole damn religion in this town."

Fargo supposed it was a natural reaction. Something terrible happens and a crowd gathers and starts to get madder than hell. And it doesn't take much from there to turn the mob violent. The trouble always is, the mob generally doesn't have all the facts, and might end up doing something as terrible—or worse—than the trouble that got them angry in the first place. There were enough of them to assault the fort and lynch Sister Salvation if they wanted to.

"For what it's worth, I don't see Sister Salvation having anything to do with this," Fargo said. "From everything I've heard, she generally sticks to hurting property, not people. Plus she'd have to know that you'd react just the way you are right now—ready to go out there and run her off. I just can't see her taking that chance."

"I can't, either," Sadler said.

"I bet Hack Heller wouldn't agree with that," somebody shouted from the middle of the crowd. "He's the real sheriff, anyway. He's the one we should be talkin' to."

Another extended rumble of agreement. Fargo

could see the pain in the old lawman's eyes. All the humiliation of the last couple years were present now—all the humiliation he'd suffered since the town council had installed Heller and Heller had, in turn, made him into his secretary.

"That's enough for now," Fargo said. "The sheriff—and he *is* the sheriff, to get that straight once and for all—has the right idea. Most of you should go on home. You've got families and work to worry about. The doc is doing everything he can."

They started falling away a couple at a time, then in groups of three and four. Within five minutes the crowd was down to eight or nine. These were women with prayer books in their hands. A few rosaries could be seen.

Fargo and the sheriff said goodnight and went back inside.

"I figured somebody'd bring up Hack," Sadler said.

"You're the sheriff. You have to remember that."

"Thanks, Fargo. I need a friend right now."

"Where the hell is he, anyway?"

"That's what I was wondering myself," Sadler said. "Heller's got a way of disappearing at odd times. He never has to explain himself to me, of course. He just disappears and then comes back and I never know where the hell he's been."

"Funny he wouldn't be around now. At a time like this, I mean."

Fargo poured them each a cup of coffee. Nodded to the door. "Wonder how it's going in there."

"Pretty much up to the Lord, now, I expect."

"I want to be out in those woods at dawn. First light'll be good enough to follow those tracks."

"Whoever it was sure had it planned out fine," Sadler said. "Stealing that horse was a nice trick."

"Well, we know that he had to be a good shot. Not great. He missed, obviously. Should've hit her right in the center, not off to the side. And we also know that he stole a horse. He had to keep it somewhere for a day. Somebody might've seen it."

"Too bad that salesman had to die," Sadler said. "Pretty sure he got a good look at the shooter."

The door to the back office opened and the doc came out. He moved like a man too exhausted to move. He was shaking his head.

Fargo waited to hear the bad news, sure to come.

But the doc said, "Don't ask me how, but she's still alive."

"What's next, Doc?" Fargo asked.

The doc snorted. "Next is I have me a little bourbon and then I start to say a lot of prayers in my own misguided way. Ain't been inside a church for thirty years and don't plan on it in the future, either. But I still remember how to pray. And that's the only weapon we got right now where poor Jane's concerned."

Then he went and got himself that drink.

Hack Heller tethered his horse in a copse of birches behind the fort and made his way to the wagon that stood by the back gate. There was little noise coming from inside. He checked his railroad watch. He was a few minutes early.

The wagon was new. The team pulling it was as tight and powerful as the wagon itself. Half an hour from now, three of the Sister's gunnies were supposed to meet Red Decker, Heller's man, and load up the wagon for the Sister. She would reward each man handsomely and then head out with a wagonful of currency rich enough to prop up the economy of a small country. She'd be taking two of the gunnies with her as far as the river, where the bags would be loaded on to a small boat. The gunnies were along to repel any of their fellow killers who might have had a mind to take all the money for themselves.

The plan was nice and easy. The one thing wrong with it was that in half an hour, the loot would all be gone. Heller and Decker would be headed away, not toward the river but rather the eastern part of the state where Heller had arranged to rent a house. He would be alone by that time, having killed Decker somewhere along the way.

There were twenty-four bags of money. Decker had hauled them from the locked shed that sat next to the rear gate. When he opened the gate for Heller, the two men would set about stealing the money. There would be no trouble from the sister's gunnies. Heller had obtained a medicine to be put in the home brew the gunnies drank every night. They would all be asleep now.

Heller checked his watch again. He had few virtues and patience sure wasn't one of them.

Molly listened to the mewling of the tiny kitten. One of the mama cats had delivered a litter three weeks ago and the kittens were already wandering around the inside of the fort. There was one especially that Molly loved. An all-white one with a black circle around the left eye and a black tip on its white tail. She had never seen a kitten like it. She had a name for it but she kept forgetting it.

Molly listened to Kate snoring. She could get pretty loud sometimes. She was loud now. She was exhausted from her day in town, talking to that Mr. Fargo. Molly wasn't sure about such things—she knew she was "slow" and that that was bad even if you didn't know what "slow" was exactly—but she had the sense that Kate had liked this Mr. Fargo more than she had admitted. The kitten. Mewling. Right outside the door.

The white one with the black circle around its eye. Molly was sure of it.

Molly whispered, "Kate. Kate."

Kate got mad—scared, really—when Molly went anywhere by herself without telling Kate first. Asking permission.

But Molly knew how tired her sister was and didn't want to wake her up. Besides, all she was going to do was go see if the kitten was all right. Molly knew what it was like to face the world all alone. That was why she was always so scared that something might happen to Kate. If Kate wasn't always there to help her—

She didn't even want to think about it.

She eased from the blankets and crawled to the front door so she could stand up. Kate and Molly slept side-by-side and if Molly stood up next to her sister, Kate would hear her for sure. And then she would say that it was night and Molly should be asleep and that she, Kate, was sure the sweet little kitten was just fine, was just mewling because it was a newborn and that was what newborns did in this world, and now it was time for Molly to get back into bed and go to sleep.

And then Molly wouldn't get to see if the kitten was all right.

Molly slipped into a coat—Kate had told her many times about being "decent" in front of other people— and slipped out to find the kitten.

12

Fargo had fallen asleep in a chair in the doc's outer office. Sadler was across the room, sleeping in a chair, too. It wasn't all that late but both men were exhausted.

Fargo dreamed of a shoot-out with Hack Heller. While he didn't think Heller had anything to do with the Connolly girls, he needed to be brought in or brought down. Despite his badge, Heller was an outlaw. There were too many like him in the West. Fargo was happy to exterminate them whenever he got the chance.

In the dream, Fargo and Heller fought with knives. They circled each other, occasionally lunging, completely wary. But the fight's odds changed significantly when Heller reached behind him and drew a pistol from the belt of his buckskins.

Dream became nightmare. Fargo realized that he had no other weapon to grab. He'd started fighting with the understanding that knives were the only weapons that would be allowed. But he'd be damned if he'd object. He didn't want to give the bigger man the satisfaction of knowing he was scared. Of knowing that his life was about to be ended.

Fargo got fancier with his footwork. It wasn't difficult to confuse Heller. Fargo lunged and Heller jumped back as if he'd been shot—jumped back though he had the clear advantage with his gun.

Fargo just kept circling.

And then Heller, grinning, raised his pistol, sighted along the barrel and prepared to send Fargo into oblivion—

When the front door opened, Fargo came awake as if somebody had thrown a bucket of ice-cold water on him. Sputtering, looking wildly around, only half-escaped from his deep sleep, he yanked his Colt from its holster.

He dropped into a gunfighter's crouch and aimed at the chest level of the silhouette in the doorway. Behind him, he heard Sadler stir.

"Well, that's not very nice, Mr. Fargo."

A woman's voice. Familiar somehow.

"You're not really going to shoot me, are you?"

"Who are you?"

Behind him, he could hear Sadler groping around for a lamp. He got it going and raised it high.

"Don't I look familiar, Mr. Fargo?" The woman smiled.

Fargo's memory strained to recognize her voice— and then realized who he was talking to. "The woman who came into my room. The maid. I mean the schoolteacher."

"Actually, I'm neither."

"You're not?"

"No. I came to town to find Sheriff's Sadler's deputy, Hack Heller."

"Why would you want to see Heller?"

"I don't want to see Heller, Mr. Fargo. Or rather I should say—I don't want to see him alive. His last job, he stuck up a short-haul train. My father was the engineer. Heller shot him to death in cold blood. No particular reason. That's just how men like him operate, I'm afraid. I came to Gladville to make sure that

Heller pays his dues, as they say. He's murdered an awful lot of people." She nodded to the doc's back office. "How's Jane Connolly doing?"

"Hanging on," Fargo said. "That's about all we know right now."

"Maybe Heller had something to do with that," she said.

"I don't see why he would," Sadler said, speaking up for the first time. "He doesn't care about Sister Salvation one way or the other."

"You may be wrong, Sheriff," she said. "My name's Margo Stacy, by the way. I've been following Heller the past few days."

"You'd better be careful, young lady," Sadler said. "No telling what he'd do if he found out that you were on his tail."

"He'd kill me. But that's not important. Three days in a row he's gone out to Sister Salvation's fort."

Fargo and Sadler glanced at each other.

"He goes into the fort?" Fargo says.

"No, he sits on a hill and watches everything through field glasses."

"But he never goes into the fort?"

"Not when I was watching him. But once a man rode out from the fort to meet him. This was at night. I got the impression the man didn't want to be seen with Heller, that they were up to something they didn't want anybody to know about."

Fargo said, "Robbery money. If everybody's right and Sister Salvation has these gunnies holding up banks and stagecoaches, she's probably got quite a cache out at the fort."

Sadler said, "And if she *does* gets robbed, she can't very well do anything about it. Not since it's money she stole herself."

"You happen to see him tonight?" Fargo asked Margo Stacy.

She nodded. In the wan light of the lone lamp, she was just as—if not more—appealing than when she'd been in Fargo's room. "I did. I followed him out to the fort again. Something's going on. There's a wagon parked by the back gate. That's never been there before."

"I wonder if Sister Salvation's getting ready to leave our little neck of the woods," Sadler said. "Maybe the wagon's for all the loot."

"And maybe," Fargo said, "this man told Heller all about the Sister leaving. And Heller decided to take the money away from her."

"Hard to believe a man of Heller's integrity would do anything like that, though," Margo Stacy said, with a gamine grin. He liked her sense of humor. "You two care to join me in a ride out to the fort?"

"I want to see what the doc says first," Fargo said. "See how Jane's doing before we leave."

Unfortunately, they didn't have to wait for the word.

Doc came out rubbing his eyes and shaking his head. He looked up at all of them and said, "No reason to stick around here any longer. I heard what you were saying about the fort. You might as well go on out there. She died a few minutes ago."

They each needed a little time to absorb what he'd said. Two sisters dead in just a couple days. But who had done it? Fargo knew he'd have to ride this whole situation down before he could leave Gladville. It wasn't rage or vengeance that gripped him now, it was a need for cold and simple justice.

"Guess we may as well head for the fort," Fargo said quietly.

They filed outside to their horses.

The robbery started two minutes late. Red Decker had taken the key from Sister Salvation's room during the dinner hour. Opening the door was easy.

Heller and Decker took two bags each from a pile near the gate. This meant fewer trips. So far, things had gone just fine.

Both men were sweating heavily. Despite the ease of the operation thus far, they kept their eyes on the sleeping fort before them. They each realized that they had very little time. Not everybody had been put to sleep with the medication. There would be strays going to the latrine every so often. One of them would almost inevitably spot what Heller and Decker were doing.

The kitten led Molly a merry chase, darting in and out between the small cabins, once even climbing up a post, beyond Molly's reach. But it had finally come down far enough for Molly to grab it. She hugged the tiny creature, enjoying the soft fur and wet nose of the kitten.

Without any warning, the kitten jumped down from her arms and went back to playing hide and seek and catch-me-if-you-can. Molly had no idea how loud she could be sometimes. Her difficulty with clear speech only seemed to exaggerate her volume.

She was desperate to find the kitten. She had one of those moments when she felt completely deserted, abandoned. Only the kitten could rid her of this sadness now. Not even seeing Kate would help. She needed the kitten.

Decker heard Molly before Heller did.

Decker was on his third trip to the wagon when some kind of ear-insulting gibberish reached his ears. It took him a moment to realize what he was hearing: Molly. Crazy Molly and that damned kitten. Molly wasn't the only one who was crazy. She'd made everybody else in the fort the same way over the past few days. She'd go looking for the tiny white kitten and, failing to find it, roam the fort bellowing for it to come to her. The thing with Molly was the louder she got, the less she enunciated. So when she was at the top of her voice, as now, you couldn't make out any of the words. Just the noise.

"What the hell is that?" Heller snapped when he came back for his last load.

"Crazy Molly," Decker explained. "She's teched."

"Yeah, well she'll wake everybody up."

And just then, she did exactly that.

A man in a nightshirt came out of his cabin about thirty yards from the shed bearing a lantern. He started walking toward Molly who, by now, was not far away from the shed herself.

"Molly, you're wakin' folks up," he said. "Does Kate know you're up?"

"I gotta find the kitty, Mr. Sayers."

Sayers wore leather boots that came halfway up his calves. They made scraping noises as he hurried to catch Molly, who had gone back to shouting for the kitten.

Sayers saw two things then: the shed door standing open and two men with guns holding bank sacks of money.

"Hey, Decker," Sayers said, "what're ya doin'? Sister give you the key or somethin'?"

Sayers had just barely completed the sentence when the huge man—the one he knew to be Hack Heller—raised a pistol appropriate to his size and fired two shots.

Molly, who was afraid of the noise firearms made, had begun screaming even before the bullets had quite ripped into Sayers' chest, blasting him backwards several feet.

"What the hell'd you do that for?" Decker cried.

"Because he woulda told everybody in the fort."

"Yeah, well take a look for yourself, Heller."

People were streaming from their small cabins, hutches and sheds. Mostly they were men and mostly they were armed. While the good Sister always insisted that guns were evil, she couldn't quite persuade men used to owning guns to give them up.

They were a ragged, comic bunch—men in nightshirts toting pistols, rifles, shotguns.

One of them broke from the pack and ran up to where Sayers lay dying.

"It's Bob Sayers!" the man cried and fell down next to his friend. "Those men shot him!"

They ran. There was nothing else to do. Ran to the wagon, pitched the last two bags into the bed and ran around to the seat.

"You take the reins!" Heller said.

"Why?"

"Because I'm a better shot than you are."

And, as if to prove it, he shot the first man through the back gate in the face.

He had to wait only a moment before the next one appeared. This one took it in the stomach. It was a terrible way to die.

Decker lashed the team with the reins and they set off.

"They're gonna come after us," Decker said.

"The hell they are. I've killed at least three of them. They won't have the nerve now. And your gunnie friends won't be awake for three or four hours yet."

"Don't fool yourself. There are more where they came from."

The conversation was ragged, barely discernible, as the wagon pounded over ground that was pitted with holes deep enough to lift the wheels off the ground.

The wagon was pounded, jounced, thrown and damn near upended as the team was lashed ever harder and plunged into the night. Heller couldn't ever remember being on ground this rough. He hadn't expected smooth riding but he sure hadn't expected this, either.

It was going to be a hell of a long and tricky ride, Heller knew. But with all the money in the back of the wagon, the discomfort would be well worth it.

13

The early French explorers had called them the Wolf People, the Pawnee who lived and thrived along this riverbank. These same French marveled when they later saw the hills. How could a land as flat as Nebraska suddenly become rocky and hilly? It was as if you'd been magically transported to a mountainous area in some faraway land.

This was the wild area that began in back of the fort, the area that Heller and Decker were preparing to hide in until the inevitable search parties tired of looking for them. The search parties would be of two kinds—legal, with the sheriff and a posse, and illegal: the gunnies from the fort wanting all that loot for themselves.

Heller's earlier plan to kill Decker had to be postponed. He'd need an extra gun for some time. If nothing else, Decker was a dangerous man with a gun.

For Decker's part, as the wagon bounced and rattled across the rocky prairie, he, too, was thinking that he wouldn't kill Heller right away. There was not only the matter of the search parties to worry about. There was also the land itself. The hilly section was something he was completely unfamiliar with. Gunnies like Decker thrived in towns, not in the wilds. Heller was also better with animals. What if one or both of the horses took sick or got injured? Decker sure as hell wouldn't know what to do.

So they piled on into the night, Heller with his thoughts of killing Decker, and Decker with similar thoughts of his own.

Fargo, Sadler and Margo rode into the shadowy night. The stage road was the best route to the fort but there was a rutted old wagon route that shaved off nearly two miles. They all wanted to get to the fort as soon as possible.

Usually by this time of night, the fort had been settled in for some time. At least a dozen coal-oil lamps and torches lit the interior of the fort. Fargo and the others sat on the hill above it. Fargo had field glasses to his eyes. Something pretty bad had happened. Three corpses were laid out in the center of the fort, and the beautiful dark-haired Kate who'd paid him a visit earlier was sobbing and shaking her head with almost frightening violence.

Fargo had the sense that whatever had happened, Sister Salvation and her people were in need of some help and weren't going to resist Fargo riding in.

"Let's see what's going on," Fargo said.

"I have a feeling Heller's been and gone," Margo said.

"Yeah, me, too."

"There are only two things he could do to escape us," Sadler said. "Either he's got a boat of some kind standing by or he's headed for those hills. If he's headed there, we're going to play hell trying to find him. You could lose an army in parts of that land up there."

"Well, let's see what happened."

As Fargo had assumed, they had no trouble getting into the fort. The front gates stood open. There was no sentry.

The three of them tied their horses to a hitching rail and walked over to where all the commotion was. Kate's sobbing was accompanied by the sobbing of two other women who knelt next to the two dead men. One of the corpses didn't have much of a face left.

Fargo went up to a woman in a cape and cowl. Her face was so lost in the shadow of the cowl that not until she raised her head did he see who he was addressing. He'd seen enough drawings of Sister Salvation around town to recognize her.

"You'd have to be Fargo," the woman said in a voice not unaccustomed to either tobacco or whiskey.

"And you'd have to be Sister Salvation," Fargo said, "the halo and all."

She smirked. "You come here to gloat, did you?"

"I came here to find Hack Heller."

"Well, then we're on the same side. I want to find him, too. He and one of my hired men, Red Decker, stole all the church's money and headed out." She nodded to the two men on the ground. "They left a couple of mementos behind." This time, her hand swept dramatically along the line of stunned men, women and children who stood in sleeping garments and coats. They were awake but it looked as if they didn't much like it. Not if this was what there was to see.

"How'd they get away without your gunnies stopping them?"

"Decker must've drugged them. They're still too groggy to be any help."

He nodded to Kate, who was being led away by two women. "What happened to her?"

"Her sister was killed by a stray bullet. One of our own men. An accident, of course, but that doesn't make it any easier." She threw back her cowl and said, "I'll make it worth your while if you go after them."

"You won't have to make it worth my while. We've all got good reasons to track down Heller, and that's what we're going to do."

"It won't be easy."

He smiled. "You talk pretty tough for a religious lady."

Her smile was as chilly as the autumn night. "You know what I am and I know what you are. No need to waste our time with insults, Fargo. That's my money and I want it back. You can take my reward or not, I don't care—as long as I get my money."

"From what I hear, a lot of banks and stagecoaches have dibs on that money before you do."

"You just bring me the money, Fargo. Then we'll argue about ownership."

A group of five men walked out the front gate. Each man carried a shovel. They weren't wasting any time burying the dead. On the frontier, with so many diseases lurking on the winds, quick burial was a good idea. In some cases, however, it was premature: the newspapers were filled with stories about people being buried alive. A fellow in Philadelphia had come up with a metal tube that stuck up from inside the coffin to a couple of inches above the ground. Apparently, it was getting popular in the East.

Sister watched them. "I'm a crusty old bitch, hard-hearted as only a whore can be. But I want you to believe one thing—one good thing—about me. I care about these people. I planned to give them a third of the money and then push on west."

"How about half for them? If you get to keep it, that is?"

She smiled. "What're you, their attorney?"

He shrugged. "Half and half just seems fairer is all."

"I'll think about it."

"First we have to get it back. And the territory we're headed into sure isn't going be easy."

"Those hills?"

"Yeah."

She winked at him. "I'll be saying prayers for you, Fargo."

As soon as she had walked away, Sadler came up. "There's a girl named Kate over there. She's getting ready to ride with us."

Fargo frowned. "I know her sister was killed, but hell, we don't want to have a caravan. The fewer the better. You get a crowd, you make yourself a target for everybody—and that includes the Pawnees we're probably going to run into."

"Be my guest, Fargo," Sadler said. "You're welcome to try and talk her out of it. But I'll lay you odds you don't."

Fargo saw how a small bit of pride and purpose had changed the sheriff into something resembling the man he must have been in his heyday. "You're enjoying yourself."

"I'm feeling like a lawman again. A real one."

Fargo clapped him on the shoulder. "Good to have you back."

Sadler nodded to the shed where Kate had lived with Molly. "She's just coming out now."

Hard to believe it was the same girl, Fargo thought. In a flat-crown black hat, a sheepskin and a pair of butternuts, she could easily be mistaken for a farm girl who'd never been blessed with a dress. The rifle was the most convincing element of her getup. Held in a gloved hand, it looked formidable. The sobbing was over. Her face beneath the hat was grim.

"Let's go," she said.

"I don't recall inviting you."

"My sister is dead. She had a bad life and a worse death. I'm going with or without you."

Fargo smiled. "There sure are a lot of folks who want to kill him."

"I'm going to make sure I get him first."

"What if he gets you first?"

She elevated the rifle so that the barrel pointed directly at the tiny white kitten that was now sitting on a fenced enclosure. Her bullet missed the animal by maybe a quarter inch, ripping up a piece of wood and flinging it into the darkness outside the glow of the nearby lantern. The kitten cried out in terror and dropped to the ground. She went to it swiftly and picked it up, planting a kiss on its head and holding it next to her face. "I was just making a point. One thing I picked up over the years was shooting. I figure I'll be able to give the bastard a good fight. If he kills me, so be it."

The virginal visage was gone; Fargo had no doubt he was looking at a delicately wrought killing machine.

As he waved everyone to their horses—and as Kate swiftly saddled up her own—Sister Salvation came over and said, "Think about that reward, Fargo. You could have an awful lot of fun with that money."

"I'll have a lot more fun catching up with Heller."

"Why can't you have both?"

He laughed. "Why, Sister Salvation, you're trying to tempt my faith."

"God helps her who helps herself."

He looked at her. "You know how some nuns give up their lives to work in leper colonies?"

She grinned. He could see that startling beauty that had once been hers. Even now she had a strong sexual pull. "Don't even talk about it, Fargo. That kind of thing gives me the creeps."

She left him to walk among her people. She was a con artist, and in some ways a ruthless one, but she certainly was not without considerable charm and wiles. She would no doubt find another group of suckers wherever she lit after this.

The people in the fort showed no signs of settling

down. Coffee and slices of bread appeared in some hands, pipes and cigarettes in others. The cabins and sheds and tents would be much warmer and more comfortable than standing out here. But close proximity to violent death agitates people as little else can. They're forced to consider their own mortality, some of them wondering when and how it will come. When their minds turn to that subject, there is no warmth or comfort to be found anywhere. Might as well stand out in the raw prairie wind as anyplace else.

Sadler said, "Maybe it'd be a good idea to have some of that bread and coffee before we go. Gonna be a long, cold night."

"All right," Fargo said. "Five minutes."

It was actually a good idea to fortify the belly. The minds were already fortified with a desire for vengeance. In Fargo's experience, a need for vengeance could get you through anything.

The bread was fresh and nourishing. The coffee had been chicoried and tasted just right. Afterward, everybody took quick turns at the latrine in back of the fort.

Then it was time to ride. They went single file out through the gates. Many of the people waved goodbye to them. Sadler's horse gave him a little trouble for no apparent reason. It took spurs to calm it down. Kate brought up the rear.

When they reached open prairie, they lined up four abreast. Because the roads were of minimal use, they set out riding hard across an endless stretch of moonlit meadow.

They soon became aware of the gently rising land. They were heading into hills heavily covered with evergreen trees.

Every one of them had the same thought as they rode: they each wanted, for a variety of reasons, to find Hack Heller.

14

Heller and Decker entered a rough area of sandstone, limestone and ragged forest that had once been the exclusive province of Pawnee hunters back in the days before they'd learned how to farm. There had been much death from starvation and disease when the nomadic Indians had had to rely only on their hunting skills to feed themselves. Hunting dogs had been a vital part of their pursuit. The land was scattered with dog bones. One of the problems with the Pawnee dogs was that their training sometimes made them mean and they fought among themselves. The dogs had also been trained as pack animals, the Pawnees tying packs to their backs. The dogs also pulled travois—two long poles with a net stretched between them. They could each carry up to seventy-five pounds.

Heller knew the land well enough to find a good hiding place for the rest of the night. One of the robberies he'd been a part of was headed up by a hunter who knew of a cave up a rutted trail that would hide a wagon of this size. They wouldn't even have to unload it. The Pawnee hunters used caves to hide, to warm their families, to store food when they settled in an area for a time. Heller had seen many caves with artifacts from centuries earlier, weapons and bones, and even drawings. They unhitched the wagon from the team so the horses could eat and rest. They pushed the wagon into the cave so nobody could see it.

Decker had brought along jerky, extra water and a few pieces of bread. They sat on the ground at the mouth of the cave eating their skimpy meal. Heller wished he'd had a good meal before he left town. He'd spent a rough life; he wanted the best things now. He didn't have dreams of fur-lined, gold-plated hotel rooms, but he did dream of comfortable, safe living in a large city where he could live the rest of his life without working, thanks to this stash of robbery money.

Then Heller started guessing about those who would be coming after him. The gunnies at the fort would just now be recovering their strength. Sadler might have found out what had happened at the fort and gotten up a posse. The only one Heller worried about was Fargo. He was capable of just about anything, if the tales told about him were true. He also had a motive to come after Heller. He'd obviously been drawn to the Connolly sisters.

Decker was prattling on about how he was going to spend his money. Heller didn't pay much attention. He stared out at the night, at the tips of the evergreens that fell just below this cave, at the waning moon and the sprawl of timbered land and huge limestone cliffs in front of them.

He considered Decker again. When and where to kill him. Not yet. Though Heller had lived in the wilds for a good share of his life, and though he was familiar with this land, the miles that lay ahead were almost eerie in their lonesome majesty. A traveling companion—even Decker—would be nice.

Decker said, "I bet that Fargo comes after us."

"Yeah? Why's that?"

"I heard that Kate back at the fort talkin' about meetin' him. She's one pretty gal. If I'm not mistaken her sister—the teched one—got killed in the shoot-out back there, or got wounded pretty bad anyway. I seen her fall. She looked dead. That's just one more reason for Fargo to sign on. And that ain't even countin' the Connolly sisters."

"I didn't kill either one of them."

"No, but he don't know that. At least not for sure. And another thing is, he got awful chummy with that sheriff."

Heller snorted. "You think I'm afraid of that old bastard Sadler?"

"Not him. But I'll bet he got Fargo to throw in with him. I'll bet Fargo's part of Sadler's posse."

The wide, circular opening of the cave was strewn with smaller rocks. Hack Heller picked one up and aimed it at Decker. It got Decker in the exact center of the forehead. You could hear bone and rock collide with furious force.

"Hey, you son of a bitch!" Decker cried out in the quiet, frosty night. Then he covered his face with his hands, the pain from the blow beginning to spread across the width of his forehead. He could feel blood beginning to trickle from the wound. "What'd you throw that rock for?"

"To shut you up. I'm sick of your talk."

"You try that again, you'll be sorry."

"Oh, yeah?" Heller laughed. "I'll be sorry, huh? Some washed-up gunny's gonna whip me, is that right?"

"If I'm such a washed-up gunny, how come you threw in with me?"

"I'm sick of your yap. Now shut up and let's catch a little sleep."

They slept, or tried to. It got cold. Sleeping on and against rock isn't a way to guarantee sleep for long. They squirmed, they resituated themselves every so often, they snored.

They didn't sleep long but they slept deep. All the excitement had taken its toll. Decker dreamed of young, fleshy women. Heller dreamed of a casino, him in fancy duds, walking around and smiling at people—an important man for the first time in his life—lookin' purty, smellin' purty.

They were lost enough in their dreams that they didn't notice the man with the Stetson, the sheepskin, the butternuts and the rifle working his way up the hill—just to the side of the trail, so he couldn't be seen. He looked just like a white man until you noticed the moccasins and the markings on them. He was a Pawnee hunter. He trapped and hunted at night, because he liked its solemnity and silence.

He had been in the underbrush when he heard the wagon coming. He climbed up into a pine and watched its passage. His eyes could not believe what he saw in the bed of the vehicle. The shape and size of the bank bags were familiar to him. He'd had many dreams of white man's money; he dreamed as feverishly about such bags as some men dreamed of sex.

They could not be too bright, these men. While white men and Pawnees tried from time to time to get along, there were no formal agreements and both sides warred on each other with some frequency. In addition to the more formal battles, men like himself roamed the wilds and God help the white men they managed to trap in places as isolated as this.

The man stood now to the side of the cave opening. The cold wind in the trees—redolent of a bitter winter already down on its way from the mountains to the west—drowned out any incidental sound he might be making.

He walked over to the big man, pointed his rifle in the man's face and then kicked him in the sole of his right boot. Hack Heller came out of his sleep half-hysterical and reaching for his gun. Why, he was gonna blow this son of a bitch away—whichever one it was; didn't matter to Hack. But just as his hand was dropping fast to his six-shooter, his one open eye recognized the fact that this was, first, an Indian son of a bitch and, second, an Indian son of a bitch with a rifle aimed right at Hack Heller's own face.

"Stand up," the Pawnee said.

"Who the hell are you?"

"Stand up."

Decker was awake now.

"Who the hell is he?"

"That's what I'm tryin' to find out."

"Both stand up; both throw down guns."

"You don't know who I am, redskin. I'm a duly God damn elected lawman."

The Pawnee was as good with one end of the gun as he was with the other. He raised his rifle and swung the butt with such force that when it reached Heller's jaw, it lifted him a full inch off the ground. Heller had probably been hit that hard a time or two but he sure couldn't recall when—not right now with blood gushing from his mouth and the inside of his lower lip feeling as if someone had slashed it with a butcher knife.

The Pawnee wasn't done. The next time he swung the weapon, the butt slammed into Heller's crotch with evil precision. Heller tried to scream but there was too much blood in his mouth—blood he was already starting to choke on.

Decker, being something less than bright, went for a knife he kept up his sleeve. The Indian put his two bullets so close to the left side of Decker's skull that all Decker could do was pitch himself to the cave floor.

The Pawnee calmly strode over, raised his moccasin, and brought the heel down precisely on Decker's knuckles. Three of them broke with a snapping sound, like dry twigs. Now he had both of them expressing misery—Heller moaning, sunk to his knees; Decker calling the Indian dirty names in a string of spitting and sputtering epithets. He kept hold of his hand tenderly, as if it were an infant that had been injured.

The Indian wasn't greedy. Nor did he want to be encumbered with a wagon. He just wanted a good deal of money. And for him, that meant taking just one of the money-stuffed bags.

He didn't have to worry about either man. They watched him with hatred so raw they almost looked comical—but mixed in with the hatred was fear. His appearance—and his violence—had been so abrupt that there was something unreal about it. Here they'd been asleep and all of a sudden—

The Pawnee went back to the wagon and began hefting the bags, trying to find the heaviest one. When he decided on one of them, he opened it up. It was just as he'd hoped. This would last him a long, long while and guarantee some very good times.

"Ain't no place you can spend that money, anyway, redskin," Decker said. "What-for you want it, anyway?"

The Indian gripped the bag and carried it over to Decker. He swung it the same way he'd swung the rifle—with no warning and with total, cold rage.

Decker's head jerked up from his former position on the cave floor when the Indian's foot contacted it; then the Indian stomped on Decker's broken knuckles.

All Hack Heller did was watch the man. Someday, sometime they'd meet up again—the crazy bastard was so stupid all he was taking was a single bag. Well, Heller certainly wasn't going to object to that.

But then the Pawnee, without a word, walked back into the cave. What was he up to?

"What the hell you doin', injun?" Decker said.

"What the hell's he doin'?" Heller said. "You got

a better look at him." It was pretty hard to understand him, the way his mouth was messed up.

"I can't tell. He's behind the wagon."

"Behind the wagon? What for?"

"How the hell would I know? He's some crazy Indian bastard is all I know."

Heller thought of going for his gun. Decker thought of going for his as well. But then the pain was on them again and they decided that it probably wasn't such a good idea. This weird Pawnee was tougher than both of them together. And that was a hell of a thing for a man to have to admit now, wasn't it?

"You figured it out yet?"

"He's squattin' down behind the wagon. That's all I can see, Heller."

A half-minute went by.

"What's he doin' now?" Heller said around all the pain and blood and swelling.

"Looks like he's—hey, you crazy injun bastard!"

Heller didn't see what was going on until it was too late. He started to get up and rush the Indian, but the Indian leveled his rifle at the unarmed Heller—and Heller jumped back.

And so the wagon went all the way down the steep trail. Clattering, clamoring, the money bags bouncing up and down.

"That's our money!" cried Decker. "We stole it fair and square!"

But that old wagon just kept rolling downhill.

15

Kate and Margo quickly befriended each other, riding side by side so they could talk whenever the opportunity came along. Kate explained to Margo how the whole experience with Sister Salvation seemed ridiculous now—as if she'd been under the Sister's spell or something. Though she kept talking about the Sister, Margo could see that the girl was only doing this to avoid talking about her poor sister, Molly. Kate was alone in the world now; Margo remembered what that was like, following the death of her father.

About two hours into their ride, the land began to rise and the landscape itself became more populated with trees of various kinds. Here and there they saw wheels from Conestogas and crosses marking burial sites—the trek westward had never been easy. Margo's family had traveled from New Hampshire to Iowa to set up farming. They'd left with eight children. By the time they got there, there were only two left. The others had died by disease, drowning, a snakebite and falling off a small cliff. The journey was perilous indeed; all that kept folks going was their belief that there was a better life and land ahead.

Margo wasn't exactly fond of the sudden timber. A perfect hiding place for somebody like Hack Heller. He might have suspected that people would chase him—had, in fact, probably just assumed they would—and so he might have doubled back to hide in the woods and begin picking them off.

Ground fog as tall as a horse had rolled in; gray clouds hid the moon suddenly and unfamiliar animal cries sawed through the silence. The stuff of nightmares.

"I have this feeling something bad's going to happen to Fargo," Kate said when they'd stopped at a creek to water and rest their horses. There was a membrane of ice on the water.

"Don't even say that," Margo said. "If something happens to Fargo, we're in very bad trouble. He's the only one who can stand up to Heller."

"How about the sheriff?"

"Oh, honey," Margo said, and touched Kate's shoulder. "Sadler's a decent man, and I'd trust him with my life. But there's no way he could stand up to Heller. You've never seen Heller in action."

"I wish I didn't have this feeling."

"Just put it out of your mind."

"Easier said than done. You know how it gets when something burrows into your brain. I wish I could just reach in there and pull it out."

Margo smiled. "Yeah, I want to do that sometimes, too. Rip out some old, bitter memory. Or some stupid plan I can't seem to get rid of." She gave the younger woman a hug. "Fargo's going to be fine. Just keep thinking that. Fargo's going to be fine and we're going to catch up with Heller and everything's going to be all right."

"I want to kill him myself."

Margo laughed. "We all want to see him dead, honey."

"He killed my sister."

"Well, honey, he killed my father."

Margo knelt down by the water and freshened herself up. The freezing water felt good on her face, revived her. She felt sorry for Kate. She still had so many illusions about life. And as they were stripped away from her one by one, she'd end up as angry as Margo felt much of the time. It seemed that so many bad people went unpunished: rich men, criminals who turned into snitches for the law, lawyers who got rich from bad people going free. Nobody cared about Heller killing her father, just as nobody cared about Heller inadvertently causing the death of poor little Kate's sister.

But for once, she thought, there was going to be a reckoning. One of the truly bad people was finally going to be brought to earth. She hadn't been kidding about each of them wanting him dead. She just hoped she got first crack.

Then she was back in the saddle and the four of them were heading out again.

The wheel tracks of the money-loaded wagon were reasonably easy to follow until the group came upon a desert-like stretch so sandy that the harsh wind had covered them up. Fargo was a good tracker and figured out that there were only two directions Heller and Decker were likely to head. And the first choice—at least if it had been Fargo doing the choosing—was the trail closest to the hills themselves. In the hills there would be caves and canyons and crevasses where two men and a wagon could hide. He led the group across the sandy stretch and then found a trail that led up into the pines.

The trail began to narrow. Fargo dropped from his horse and saw signs of the wagon wheels again. Somewhere up in the hills above them Hack Heller waited.

Since he rode lead, he turned around and signaled for the three others to stop. He walked back to them. "Unless I'm misreading the signs, Heller's somewhere up in that cluster of hills. If we go much farther all together, he'll hear us coming."

Then thunder rumbled down the sky. Dawn had been wan, gray. Easy now to see why: thunderheads clouded the sun. You could taste and smell the rain that was about to start.

Fargo nodded to the heavy pines on either side of the trail. "You three can keep warm and dry under those trees."

"No; you're not going alone, Mr. Fargo. I'm going with you."

Fargo might have expected this from Margo but not from Kate.

Margo said, "I was just about to say I'd go with you, Fargo. No offense, Kate but I'm a little older and a little more seasoned. Why don't you wait here with the sheriff?"

Sadler laughed. "I was going to say *I'd* go with you, Fargo. But it looks like you're a pretty popular man."

Fargo shrugged. Taking Sadler along would leave the women unprotected, which is why he preferred to work alone. "One of you two ladies can go, but not both of you. Like I said, Heller knows what he's doing. Even if we're as quiet as we can be, he's going to hear three of us. That's just the way it is."

"Please," Kate said to Margo, "I want to be there when Heller's caught."

"You think I don't, Kate? I've got the same rights you do. In fact, I've got more rights, seeing as how Heller killed my father directly."

Kate looked at Fargo. "How'll we ever decide this?"

Sadler said, "How about the old-fashioned way?"

"And what would that be?" Margo said dubiously.

"By flipping a coin. That should be easy enough." Sadler dug into the pocket of his sheepskin. "Got one right here."

"Is this all right with you, Mr. Fargo?" Kate said.

"Anything's fine with me as long as we get going."

"Flip the coin, sheriff," Margo said. "I'll call it when it's in the air."

Sadler took off his leather glove. Set the coin on his thumbnail. Brought his index finger close. Flipped.

"Heads," Margo said just as the coin soared into the air.

"I guess that leaves me tails," Kate said, sounding as if she'd been tricked or cheated.

All of them watched the coin go up. Rain began to spatter now. This was going to be a hard, cold rain.

The coin came down and slapped the top of Sadler's hand. "Tails."

Margo made a face. "I still don't think it's fair. He personally killed my father. He didn't personally kill her sister."

"That was a fair flip," Fargo said.

He went to his horse and took the few things he'd need. The rain was slashing the pine trees now. The wind was getting stronger.

"We'll be back," Fargo said.

They set off. For a while they could still hear Margo complaining.

"I'm sorry if I hurt her feelings," said Kate.

"It was her feelings or yours and the flip was fair."

"I really do want to kill him, Mr. Fargo."

"Do me a favor and stop calling me 'Mr. Fargo.' I feel like your uncle."

He was surprised to see her blush. "Oh, that's not the way I think of you at all, Mr.—Skye. Not at all, believe me."

He smiled. "Good."

They quickly reached an even narrower point on the trail where the pines grew almost together, giving them a pretty decent roof to walk beneath. The rain poured; there was a real violence to it. You could hear the dismayed, even frightened forest creatures scurrying for cover, for respite.

Up the ever-steeper hill they went. They had not reached the base of the hills that soared above this small foothill they were on. That would change when they reached the second level of terrain. Heller would have a clean look at them if they stayed on the trail then. They would have to go off-trail and begin sneaking their way up.

Kate almost fell backward at one point. He turned around quickly and grabbed her hand. He steadied her. Her hand was still in his. It filled him with quick, explosive desire. He had to keep his mind on the task at hand. Had to.

But he sensed Kate had felt it, too. In attempting to break her fall, she'd slid her arm around his waist. She seemed reluctant to let go now. "Thanks, Skye."

"My pleasure."

It was sort of odd, all that was going on—all the death, and the rain a damn downpour by this time— to just be standing there holding each other like that.

Fargo said, "Maybe we'd better keep going."

"Yeah."

But even so, they didn't move. Not quite yet. Just one more lingering moment. Then he realized that he was going to do something foolish if he didn't force himself to turn around and resume their climb.

"C'mon," he said.

"Do we have to?"

He grinned. "Yeah. We have to."

They had to crouch to move off-trail. The pine boughs hung low—way too low to stand up under. Not only did they not want to be seen on the trail, but it was dry enough under the boughs to keep their weapons from harm.

It wasn't long before the climb started to feel endless. This hill was deceptive. All the pines tended to minimize the look of the actual slope. But it was steep enough and long enough for them to get winded—winded enough that when they took an occasional break there was no hand-holding or thoughts of *amore*. Hard to think of lovemaking when your breath was coming out in gasps.

When they finally reached the top of the hill and the small piece of sandy soil between it and the much taller one ahead, Fargo stopped.

He had to consider the possibility that this was leading nowhere. That Hack Heller wasn't going to be anywhere near here. The wagon tracks hadn't been all that distinct. Maybe they were tracks that belonged to somebody else entirely.

The Trailsman didn't like self-doubt. He wasn't one of those swaggering morons who just assumed that every hunch he had was the right one. But on the other hand he wasn't one of those overly cautious second-guessers who paralyzed themselves with indecision.

The tracks had definitely been Heller's up until they'd reached that desert-like stretch. When they'd picked up the tracks again—this owing to the rockier terrain—the tracks became harder to read. But they were still reasonably fresh. What were the chances of another wagon coming along in the middle of the night? Slim to none.

She came up to him, not sliding her arm around his waist, but sliding her arm through his. "Is there a reason you're standing out here in the pouring rain?"

He laughed. "Hell, I didn't even notice. I guess I still thought I was under the pine boughs. I must have got lost thinking about things."

"Well, how about we get under the boughs again while that giant brain of yours figures things out? We're both wet enough already."

"Not a bad idea."

This time when they got under the boughs, he sat cross-legged against a tree and managed to roll a cigarette with his wet hands.

"Can I have a puff?"

"You're too young."

"I'm nineteen."

"That's too young."

She grinned and slapped him playfully on the arm. "C'mon. I used to sneak puffs all the time."

He grinned back. "Well, all right, old-timer. Just be careful not to put the lighted end in your mouth."

"Very funny."

She took a surprisingly large and surprisingly deep drag off the cigarette and then exhaled in a heavy blue plume of smoke. "That tasted good. Tobacco always does. Even when it stings a little."

He reached for the cigarette but she said, "One more," and gave herself another pull.

After she'd exhaled, she took the cigarette and expertly dislodged the red coal at the tip of it, the way folks do when they want to save the rest of the cigarette for later.

"Hey," Fargo said, "what're you doing?"

"What I'm doing, Skye," she said, no longer the shy religious girl but someone with a throatier voice and far more self-possession, "is trying to forget everything but right here and right now because if I don't, I'll go on a crying jag that'll never stop."

And without any further notice, she took him in her arms and kissed him with a fervor that made him feel ten years younger. He was also pretty sure that smoke was coming out his ears.

She eased her arms around the back of his neck and then pulled him down on top of her. They were both bundled up pretty well but they didn't let that slow them down. Their mouths connected and her tongue began to stir him to a level of pleasurable insanity. In one moment, his hands had slipped up under her shirt. Her breasts were perfectly formed, the nipples large and erect. The moment he touched them, she began pressing her loins against him in a frenzy that matched his own.

Then she was slipping out of her clothes entirely, somehow managing to do this without withdrawing her tongue from his mouth. The feel of her nakedness, especially of the warmth between her legs, brought his own surging steel to an almost painful level of urgency. Though he was hardly aware of it, she was stripping his trousers down to his boots, and then working one trouser leg off at a time.

He eased his way down her pale, sumptuous body till he reached the place of her ultimate pleasure and there he tasted of her tangy splendor. She bucked, she threw herself from side to side, she grabbed his ear and prompted his tongue in deeper, faster. Her strength surprised him—maybe it even surprised her— as she steered and maneuvered his head to guide him to exactly the right position.

He knew she would scream her pleasure, so he clamped his hand on her mouth as she delivered her wild, hip-thrashing joy to the world.

He let her enjoy every millisecond of her passion. And then her hand was on him and she was pulling him up, up and inside her where they quickly found a mutual rhythm, him beginning slowly but gradually starting to thrust, deeper and faster as she once again climbed to the pinnacle.

His lovemaking only grew in urgency. He filled his hands with her buttocks and began to grind their bodies until they were virtually one.

She was with him completely, lifting and falling in time with him, her own hands on his buttocks now, urging him on as he urged her.

And then it was done.

He hung there in that spent, dizzy, dark, perfect moment of completion, lost in all-time all-space—no other life experience like it—until reality in the form of her body, the rain-dripping pine boughs and the soughing wind brought him back to the present.

The chill day started to dry his sweat.

He brought her to him, kissed her cheek.

He could see that she was going to start crying about her sister again. He hugged her. "C'mon, we'll go find Heller."

"Just remember," she said between sniffles, "I'm the one who gets to kill him."

16

"I ever get my hands on that sonofabitch Indian," Hack Heller said.

"Yeah, I know, you're gonna hang him."

"I'm gonna burn him first. Set him right on fire and watch him suffer."

"I'd rather gut-shoot him and leave him to die."

"Gut-shoot him and cut his eyes out."

"Gut-shoot him, cut his eyes out and saw off his nose."

There was nothing like a busted-up wagon to put two killers in a foul mood. When the Pawnee had shoved the wagon down the hill, he either did so with great precision and skill, or he was just the luckiest Indian in a five-thousand-square-mile radius.

The wagon with all the money in it—all the money, of course, except the lone bag the Pawnee had stolen—had veered off the path and hit a tree head on. A big-ass tree. A *huge*-ass tree. Meaning that the front of the wagon was stove in and had to somehow be fixed without any tools, any extra lumber or any special expertise on hand. Here were two men who could shoot, steal, burn, stab, stomp, rape, lynch and cheat with the best of them—renaissance men in their own scabrous way. But carpenters they weren't.

The first thing they had had to do was empty the

wagon bed of money sacks so they could push the wagon back on to the trail. That was the easy part. Then came the part of grunting, groaning, cursing and shouldering the wagon back up the hill to where the horses were so they could travel on from there. Hack Heller wasn't sure where they were going; he just knew that they had to keep pushing away from the posse that was almost certainly on their trail.

It took half an hour to get the wagon back up to the team. Then they spent twenty minutes just looking at the front of the wagon. The seat and floor were smashed right up the middle, looking like an inverted V. One option was to pull out the damaged section so that it was flush again, but the wood might break in two. Another option was just tearing the whole section off—just sit on the edge of the seat-shorn wagon and run the reins from there. There was a third option, too, and that was to just leave it as it was and make do.

Which is what they'd pretty much decided to do until Decker happened to notice the left rear wheel.

"Son of a bitch," he said.

"What's wrong?"

"C'mere."

Heller went.

"That don't make no sense," Decker said, pointing to the problem.

"It sure don't."

And it didn't.

You run a wagon down a hill into a tree head-on, you expect the damage to be limited to the front end of the vehicle. If you get very unlucky, something happens to one of the two front wheels.

What you don't expect—what makes no sense whatsoever—is for the left rear wheel comes loose.

"Now how the hell could that happen?" Heller said.

"The back wheel. I'll be."

The left rear wheel was at an angle, giving every indication that it would fall off if it was moved a few feet.

"At least we can fix it," Decker said.

"We can?"

"I know a little bit about wheels. I used to steal wagons from farmers."

Heller smiled. "You just never know what's gonna come in handy, do you?"

You could see Decker was real proud of himself, knowing about wagons and all.

He got down on his haunches and started jabbing and poking and knuckling and prodding around on the cap of the axle and going "hmm" and "lookee here" and "uh huh"—things that a wagon man would be likely to say, putting on a show for old Hack Heller, who was standing right behind him.

As it turned out, it wasn't the jabbing or the poking or the knuckling or the prodding that got Decker— who really didn't know beans about wagons or wheels or axles—in trouble.

It was when he put both hands on either side of the perilously slanted left wheel and gave it just the teeniest, tiniest nudge, at which point the entire left side of the wagon collapsed and the wheel rolled free. Well, he thought, at least it hadn't broken in half.

Heller kicked him in the back with such force that Decker slammed head-first into the collapsed wagon and raised a nice blue egg on his forehead.

Sheriff Dave Sadler hadn't minded staying behind. Not at first, anyway. Though he'd been enthusiastic about chasing his former deputy and paying him back for all the indignities the big man had put upon him, the cold weather and the rain had begun to wither him. He needed to stop, to catch a bit of sleep, to just plain rest for a time.

The pines gave him plenty of shelter once he got used to angling himself in a certain way so that the branches kept out all the rain. He tried to stay awake but couldn't.

Margo listened to him snore and smiled. Her father had snored like that. The family used to make jokes about how much noise he made while he slept. When she was very little, she liked to climb into the cot where her mother and father slept. It was a privilege seldom granted. There were three kids and her parents had been scrupulous about taking turns with the honor.

She felt sorry for poor old Sadler. It was embarrassingly obvious that he was trying to win back his self-respect—be the hard, fast lawman that he'd once been. But time and Hack Heller had taken their toll. In a certain light, you could see that Sadler's skin had turned a waxy yellow color, and his eyes—though she didn't think he drank much—were always weary with streaks of bright red.

Crouching down was making her sleepy herself. She'd thought of waking him up, taking her turn at snoring up the place. She'd even started to crawl over to him but then stopped. He needed his sleep a lot more than she needed hers.

So she sat, contented. Every once in a while, she'd notice a squirrel or a possum or a raccoon come up to a nearby tree and take a gander at who had invaded its territory. There was a whole world in here, Margo thought, as she sat under the pines on the slick needle floor. She was snug and reasonably warm, even with the endlessly slashing rain.

Then she felt pressure. She needed to empty her bladder. She'd had more than her share of water earlier on.

She could go right here, of course. Sadler hadn't stirred in some time and it wasn't likely he would any time soon.

But what if he did? There she'd be, crouched down in a familiar pose, and his eyes would fly open and she'd give him an uneasy grin and feel like a fool.

No, the best thing to do was to haul herself across the trail and relieve herself in the trees.

She didn't worry much about being a proper lady. But she didn't like to put herself in foolish positions, either.

She listened a few more minutes to the grand opera Sadler's snoring had become and then decided to work her way over to the trail and stand up. Stretching would feel good. Emptying her bladder would feel even better.

No trouble reaching the trail. No trouble standing up and stretching. No trouble enjoying thirty seconds of the rain, the chill of which revived her.

No, the trouble came in another form.

Unless she was mistaken—this could always be part of a dream, she told herself—there was a man standing about three feet from her with a Colt in one hand and a bag of bank money in the other. He was a red man, a Pawnee, she supposed, and he had a face that was a knife slash of cold anger. She sensed that he hated just about everybody—especially just about everybody who happened to be white.

If he minded the downpour, he didn't let on.

He walked over to her and put the barrel of the gun in the center of her forehead. "Want woman."

His voice was actually sort of high-pitched, when compared it with the low-pitched rage in his eyes. If somebody was playing him in one of those "meller-dramas" her various beaus took her to from time to time—well, they'd get an actor with a deeper voice.

But then this wasn't a "meller-drama," now was it?

She suddenly felt wretchedly sorry for herself.

Why did her father have to die? Why did she have to stand out here and get soaked? She was already getting a scratchy throat. Why did a terrifying, angry Pawnee have to come along with rape in his eyes? She had no doubt that that was what his two words signified. And why on top of all these things did she have to go to the toilet so badly? That just made all the other things that much worse. But then, would this Pawnee who not only wanted to rape and possibly kill her—would he understand the words she'd use for "bladder" or "toilet"?

She put her hands up in the air and squatted down, indicating by pointing to a spot between her legs what she needed to do.

At first, he just stared at her with his quiet fury. But after she kept pointing for a while, recognition dawned on his face.

He smiled. Actually smiled. And had a nice smile, too.

He smiled and then he laughed—well, chuckled anyway—and then he pointed to a place off-trail where she could go and do her business.

She felt ridiculously grateful to him.

As her bladder level was lowering, she started trying to figure out how she was going to kill him before he raped and or killed *her*.

And where the hell had he picked up that bank bag, anyway?

When Fargo reached the top of the small hill, he was able to see the ever-larger hills above him. Heller and Decker could be anywhere in there. Or maybe nowhere.

By this time, his clothes were so soaked he scarcely noticed the rain any more, except when he was silent long enough to hear it drumming on top of his hat and bouncing off the brim.

Kate was struggling behind him, slipping on the now-muddy trail while trying to keep from dropping her rifle. He pitied Heller when they all caught up with him.

"Could we just get out of the rain for a little while?" she said.

"Sure."

He'd been thinking the same thing himself but she'd beat him to it. Even though he was getting accustomed to the downpour, it had started to create the kind of muddy trail that could easily break a leg. Treacherous was the word, particularly when you were traveling uphill.

They ran over to a shallow copse of pine trees and sat themselves down under it. She was shivering. He put his arm around her and held her.

"We used to come up here and explore," she said, teeth chattering.

"Who did?"

"Molly and I."

"You ever find anything interesting?"

"Not especially. But it was fun."

"I'm surprised Sister Salvation let you go this far."

"Well, she didn't exactly know."

He laughed. "In other words, you snuck out."

"Yeah, I guess you could say that. But we had to go real early because to get here and back to the fort before dark took a long time. We had to kind of scout things out over several trips. We couldn't ever stay long enough to cover even half of it at a time."

"So nothing interesting, huh?"

"Well, it's beautiful land." She sneezed with some violence. "When it's not pouring down freezing rain, it's beautiful, anyway." Then she smiled to herself. A memory. "A bear came after us once. That was the most excitement. People didn't believe us. They said there weren't any bears in this area. Well, this was definitely a bear. Maybe he was just vacationing here. But he was a real bear and a big one, and he chased after us."

"What did you do?"

"Well, there're a couple of hills where there're a lot of caves. Thank God we were near there when the bear came after us. We went far back in this one cave and there was this crawl space. The bear came in after us but it couldn't fit into the crawl space. So we stayed there for a real long time. But we still managed to make it back to the fort by dark. We were a little late but we just told Sister Salvation that we'd gotten lost while we were mushroom hunting. She wouldn't have believed us about the bear. She didn't mind when we hunted mushrooms in this woods."

Her reference had moved right on past him. But then, after she finished speaking and sneezed once again, he realized he should ask her about it.

"You mentioned these caves?"

"Yeah. Those two hills are full of them. It's like they're stacked on top of each other, from the bottom of the hill to the top. You can't see them all because the trees hide them. But they're there, all right. Molly and I spent all our time there one day, just going up and down and counting the caves. There were something like sixteen of them. Various sizes."

"Are we anyplace near them?"

She thought a moment. "Well, not really near. But then not really far."

"Thank you. That's very helpful."

She giggled. "I just mean it wouldn't take us very long to get there if it wasn't raining."

"It'd be a good place to hide out. . . . Big enough to put a wagon inside?"

"I think so. A couple of them are that big, anyway."

"Well, we sure haven't come up with much in this direction."

"Probably wouldn't take a half-hour. Well, maybe an hour. But we'd be soaked."

"We're soaked now."

She sneezed again. Smiled. "I guess that's a good point."

Where am I?

Dave Sadler woke with a start. Instantly he felt like a doddering old fool. His old man used to get disoriented that way. Would get up and spend the first five minutes just babbling, saying all kinds of crazy stuff.

Sadler didn't know where he was. He was ashamed of this and afraid of it—had his mind taken some kind of terrible and irretrievable turn?

Something had wakened him. He couldn't remember exactly. Something . . . jarring. A sound. He began to catalog the sounds around him. Hard rain. Raindrops crackling on pine branches. Wind. Strong wind.

Then smells: pine, wet earth, his own damp clothes.

And then he remembered: Fargo and Kate going on up into the hills. Margo and he staying down here. Margo. He then remembered the sound that had awakened him. A scream. Margo's scream. He was sure of that.

When he'd dozed off, Margo had been sitting next to him. Where had she gone? What had caused her to scream?

His six-gun. He touched his side. Felt the butt of the gun riding there.

And then it came again: Margo's scream. Muffled by the rain and the wind. But distinct enough for him to identify it as Margo's. And to recognize the fact that she was in some kind of terrible trouble.

He stood up sharp and quick and banged his head against a low-hanging branch. His hat absorbed most of the punishment. He bent low so he could move fast beneath the canopy of branches. When he reached the trail, he listened hard for any sound other than wind and rain, but heard nothing.

He started walking down the path when he heard a

male voice say something loud but not articulated enough for Sadler to understand.

Off the other side of the trail was where it came from. The pines branches interlaced, the trees grew so close together. No path whatsoever. All he could do was plunge into the wall of trees ahead of him.

The old excitement—heady, almost overwhelming—filled his entire body. He was ten years younger. Fifteen years younger.

Whip that gun out, you old bastard. Find the girl. Save the girl. You used to save girls all the time, from perils of every kind.

Sure wasn't an easy passage, this kind of deep timber. Might as well be in a cave, some parts of this were so dark and overgrown. Stumbling, grabbing on to a bough for support, letting the branches lash his face. No point in fighting any of it. Just do the best he could.

Then something strange happened. A while ago it had been Margo screaming for help. But this time it was a man screaming. And—if Sadler interpreted the intent of that scream—now the man was pleading for help. He was pleading in Pawnee, a language Sadler knew only slightly.

If a Pawnee buck had attacked Margo, why was the buck crying out for assistance? None of it made a hell of a lot of sense.

He staggered out from between two trees into a small, oval clearing. And then he understood why the Pawnee was screaming for help.

Margo's clothes had pretty much been torn from her body. Her face showed bruises even through the blinding rain. The blood streaming from her had been quickly washed away.

But the Pawnee had gotten the worst of it because Margo had him on the ground, his wrists tied behind him. She had used her kerchief for his wrists. She was using her belt for his ankles. He kept kicking and rolling but every thirty seconds or so, tired of him trying to elude her, she'd take her knife and stick it right above his eye. That calmed him down considerably. He realized that if he moved too quickly, he could jerk the blade right into his own eye.

Sadler, amazed, walked up to her. "You all right?"

"I am now." She looked up through the rain. "He had his knife at my throat and was going to rape me. But then I kicked him a good one right between the legs and he hasn't been the same since." She reached down and eased the knife point just a wee bit closer to his eyeball.

"Hey," Sadler said, finally spotting the bank bag. "He must've gotten that from Heller."

"Yeah," Margo laughed. "Which means he can tell us where Heller *is.*"

17

The rain had given out a while ago. By then, Fargo and Kate had reached the section of hills where the caves were.

"I guess there were more caves than I remembered," Kate said.

Plenty of caves, all right. There was one hill that had so many caves it looked liked a hotel, each cave a room for the weary traveler. There were other caves that the Pawnee had hidden behind shrubbery of various kinds. But the rain had disturbed the coverings enough that at least some of the caves could now be seen.

In other words . . .

"I guess this is going to take longer than I thought, Skye," Kate said. "I guess I was having so much fun with Molly that I didn't pay any attention to all these other caves. We had our own special ones."

"There's another problem."

"What's that?"

"If Heller's up there somewhere and he sees us, he'll cut us down for sure. We'll stick together and stay in the pines as much as possible. If there's a cave that's out in the open with no cover, I'll check that one out by myself."

"And what happens if he isn't there?"

"Then we've wasted a lot of time."

So they set off. Despite the clean, fresh air and the heady scent of pine, the ill effects of the rain lingered on. Walking was slow business in the mud and muck.

This first hill was pretty easy to survey. There were eight, nine caves at most, and even from a distance Fargo could see that they wouldn't be much of a hiding place for a wagon. Just not enough room.

The second hill took more time. There were three good-sized caves there. Each had to be approached carefully, guns drawn. But they proved to be cold and empty, the only traces of human life being the remains of fires built by woodsmen or Pawnee.

When they'd set off, Fargo had felt pretty optimistic that Heller had put into one of the caves. You couldn't drive a wagon very far in the downpour they'd had. You'd get stuck for sure. So what else could you do but put in somewhere?

But now he began thinking that maybe Heller had managed to beat it around these hills before the rain and was now hiding out in a cabin somewhere miles ahead. The picture of Heller sitting with his feet up on a table, a cigar in the corner of his mouth, a glass of good bourbon in his hands, and piles of bank sacks on the table in front of him tended to rile the Trailsman up a bit.

He didn't say any of this to Kate, of course. She didn't need any more discouragement. Every once in a while he'd heard her behind him or beside of him choking on angry tears. Molly. Kate had clearly devoted her life to the girl. Hadn't had time for men or even herself. Took up with Sister Salvation because she felt that such a true calling could not only bring her closer to God but could also help Molly in some way. And now Molly had been taken from her. And in the last several hours she'd been forced to march through a brutal storm—soaked, despondent, afraid of what lay ahead, wanting only to kill Heller.

Fargo took a break between caves to stretch his back and have a cigarette. There were just so many places to look in these hills. Heller wasn't cooperating. If he just built a fire or shot off a couple of rounds. One thing about bad guys, Fargo had noticed. They weren't very helpful when you were tracking them down. Ungrateful bastards.

Kate came over and bummed a couple of drags off his cigarette. "What happens when it gets dark?"

"I marked our trail. We go back down and find Sadler and Margo."

"They're probably wondering if we're still alive."

"It's probably worse than that."

"Huh?"

He smiled. "They're probably bored to death. Sitting in one place for four hours isn't a hell of a lot of fun."

Fargo ground the cigarette out carefully. Even with all the wet earth, he had to be careful of wildfires.

"Well, c'mon," he said. "We'll check out a few more."

"I was hoping I'd have shot and killed him by now."

"That's the trouble with things like this," Fargo said. "It's ninety-nine parts drudgery to one part fun."

"I'll forget all about the drudgery when I kill him. That's the only part I'll remember, Skye," she said in that soft, mannered little voice of hers. "Killing him, I mean."

It took some convincing of the physical variety, but finally the Pawnee began to speak in broken English. Sadler had given the man his choice: talk or die.

They stood in the path—Margo, Sadler and the Pawnee who said his name was Two Owl. He said he had been hunting in the hills when he came upon the wagon and the two sleeping men. "Your people have stolen many things from us. I thought I would steal something from you."

Margo smiled. "You're right, Two Owl. But there are bad men on both sides. The men with the wagon—they stole this money. And killed many people, too."

"That is white people's business," Two Owl said. "With that money I could buy much for my people."

"We have to give the money back," Dave Sadler said. "It belongs to a bank. I'm sorry, Two Owl." He laughed. "I wouldn't mind keeping a little of that myself." Then, the lawman stirred in him again. "I want two things from you. The first is to apologize to Margo here for trying to rape her and the second is for you to lead us to this cave where the wagon is. It can't have gotten far in that rain. It's probably still there now. With night coming and all."

"She is a white woman," Two Owl said. "No apology."

"You have a wife?"

"Yes. A beautiful one."

"What if I tried to rape her?"

"I would kill you."

"Well, there you have it, Two Owl. I don't want to have to kill you. But I do want you to apologize."

Two Owl sighed. "I will say the words."

Margo said, "Meaning you'll say the words but not mean them."

"Whites rape many of our women. Kill many, too."

"Like I said, Two Owl," Sadler said, "there are plenty of bad people on both sides. Now you go ahead and say it."

Two Owl looked at Margo and frowned. "You are strong woman. You stopped me."

"That's not an apology," Sadler said.

Two Owl shrugged. "I am sorry."

Sadler looked at Margo. "Good enough?"

Margo rolled her eyes. "It'll have to be. I doubt a white man would apologize to him. He feels the same way about us. We're not going to settle anything here today. He'll go away hating whites and we'll go away being leery of Indians."

"I suppose you're right."

"Good enough?" Two Owl said, imitating Sadler.

Margo couldn't help it. She laughed. "Yes, Two Owl. Good enough."

Sadler said, "We need you to lead us to the cave?"

"I want money."

Sadler sighed. "Two Owl, this isn't my money to give. It belongs to a bank."

"Money," Two Owl said.

Now it was Sadler's turn to laugh. "You steal money, you nearly rape a woman, and now you want some kind of reward?"

"Money," Two Owl said.

Sadler shook his head, thought a moment. "Tell you what. If we bring all the money back, I'll see to it that the bank gives you some kind of reward. You know what a reward is?"

"How much?" Two Owl said.

"I'd say he knows what a reward is," Margo smiled.

"I can't say for sure," Sadler said. "But I'll get you as much as I can."

Sadler was getting a headache. If he ever needed anybody to represent him in a business transaction, he'd get Two Owl. The other side would give in just because Two Owl was so mercenary and implacable.

"Let's get going," Margo said.

"We need you to lead us to the cave. Can you do that?"

Two Owl's eyes scanned the trees on the west side of the trail. "There is a way to save time but it is a rough path. I'm not sure you could make it. An old man and a girl."

"You don't worry about us, Two Owl," Margo said, hating to be relegated to being "a girl." "I'll make it just fine. And so will the sheriff here."

"There will be many animals in the night," Two Owl said. He was obviously trying to scare them and taking great delight in doing so.

Margo said to Sadler, "I'll bet he tells great campfire stories."

Sadler grinned. "Yeah, I'll bet he does, too."

"So can we go now?" Margo said to Two Owl. "We're worried about our friends. We want to make sure they're all right."

"Many animals in woods," Two Owl said.

"Uh huh," Margo said.

And so they finally set off.

Sadler just hoped Fargo and Kate were still alive. They'd been gone a long time.

By the time Hack Heller finished repairing the wagon—righting the wheel, setting up the smashed front so that it would be useful rather than a hindrance—his hands were wounds. This kind of work required skill and a certain amount of sensitivity. Heller applied the "battering" method. It worked—at least for now. At dawn, they'd pull out. With all their money. Heller would, anyway. He figured on killing Decker in his sleep tonight.

Heller was convinced that two of the money bags were missing. One, the Pawnee had taken. But the other—it had to be somewhere on the short trail the wagon had hurtled down after the Pawnee had given it a shove. There was a good moon, so Heller went looking.

The early evening was downright cold. All the trees and undergrowth were still heavy with rain. His arms got all soaked again just looking through the underbrush.

Heller just kept thinking of what lay ahead for him. He would make some life for himself—the kind of life most men only dream of. Hack Heller, a man among men. There was one other thing: Out here in the sticks, he always dragged his reputation with him. But out in the far west—nobody knew who he was.

He listened carefully to the night sounds. Pawnee used a lot of bird signals to talk back and forth. To the untrained ear they weren't meaningful or especially interesting. Just birds yakking.

There was a possibility that the lone Pawnee who'd made off with the bank bag had told others about the cache of cash in the cave. This pine forest could be filled with Pawnee right now. He listened even more intently.

He had spent half an hour on his search before he heard them coming. At first he had no idea who they were or what they were doing. Could be completely innocent—town-types somehow lost in the pines—but the more he thought about that, the more he realized that there could be nothing innocent about it. Town-types with no bad intent in their hearts would have turned back as soon as the rain had let up.

No, this would probably be one of the raiding parties the Pawnee intruder had tipped off about the wagon-load of cash.

He moved as quietly as possible. He wanted to continue his search while listening for them to draw closer. He now just assumed it was an Indian raiding party.

He found the bag fifteen minutes after he first became aware of the group moving near him. The bag lay just off the trail, under a thorny covering of undergrowth. He reached it and pulled it out. The thorns were sharp as snakebites.

He had been going to wait for the raiding party here. No longer. He had the bag. Why not use the cave and the newly repaired wagon for cover? They would have to assault the cave and in doing so a number of them would die quickly. There was only one entrance to the cave and you could squander an awful lot of lives trying to get in that way.

Decker—always a big help—had already dozed off for the evening. He didn't wake up until Heller stood over him.

"Pawnee on the way, Decker. Get your ass up."

"How you know about Pawnee?"

"I could hear them coming."

"If you could hear them coming, they ain't Pawnee."

"Yeah, well I say they are. Anyway, how the hell would you know? You were asleep."

"Just had my eyes closed was all. Restin'."

"You lazy bastard, I said 'get up' and I mean it."

Decker stood up. "I could get real tired of you pushin' me around."

"We'll settle this up later. Right now we got Pawnee to contend with. Let's drag the wagon in front of the cave, block the entrance. We can fire from behind it."

"How many you think there are?"

"Can't tell for sure. Not that many."

"Still bothers me," Decker said, "that they're makin' enough noise to be heard. Pawnee know how to move around without you knowing anything about it till it's too late."

They moved the wagon in front of the cave. They pushed all the bank bags to the rear of the wagon. This way they had room to lie down in the bed of the wagon and could fire from their prone positions. Heller didn't plan on offering any conversation to the Indians. He'd just open fire when he first got wind of them.

Then the familiar mixture of boredom and fear set in upon the two men. It sure was dull lying here. You could wait for them for a long time. There was at least a possibility that Heller had misread the situation. There was at least a possibility that Heller had been wrong in the first place. No Pawnee at all. Simply some lost and luckless white travelers who were trying to work their way out of these woods.

This was what Decker tried to tell himself, anyway. But somehow he knew better.

18

Two Owl thought that he had never heard noisier people in his life than Sheriff Sadler and the white woman named Margo. They might be brave, they might be good fighters, they might even be skilled with knives in addition to firearms—Two Owl was willing to concede all this.

What he was not willing to concede was their ability to move secretly through terrain of any kind. It didn't matter if they were on clear trail or in dense forest. It didn't matter that she couldn't have weighed much more than a hundred pounds. Or that, given his age, Sadler walked quietly.

The two of them together made as much noise as an army.

When they'd first set off, he had spoken to them angrily about all the noise they were making. He had reasoned with them—why alert anybody and everybody to their presence? Was stealth something they'd never heard of before?

Apparently, the answer to that was yes. *Tramp, tramp, tramp; whisper, whisper, whisper; tramp tramp tramp*. The strange—almost comic—thing was that they really had cut down on their noise. But it was so loud to begin with that it was *still* loud even now that it was subdued.

Why didn't they just break out in song? That way anybody in the timber would know they were there.

Two Owl heard sounds just as the three of them were headed back in the direction of the trail. From here, he couldn't be sure who it was or what they were up to. He knew they were white. At the moment, that was all his ears told him.

Minutes later, Sadler said, "Sssh. I hear something."

Two Owl almost smiled. It took longer for whites than Indians to hear "the words of the words," a language that took many forms, from drums to imitations of animals. But the old man had finally heard the noise that had been disturbing Two Owl for some time now.

"I don't hear anything," Margo said.

"Sssh," Sadler said again.

Time to move, to act, Two Owl thought.

He turned to the two behind him.

"You wait here."

"For what?" Margo said. "That's all I've been doing all day long. Waiting. I'm sick of it."

He was so exasperated he didn't bother to tell her she was making too much noise. Voices carried, in case she didn't know.

"You hear it, too?" Sadler asked.

"Hear what?" Margo said.

"Later I will tell you," said Two Owl. "For now stay here and don't talk."

"Maybe you're just going to run away," Margo snapped.

"Tell her, lawman."

"He heard something," Sadler explained to her. "So did I. But I reckon he heard it a long time before I did. He's got a lot better ears for this kind of thing."

Sadler checked his six-shooter.

Margo checked hers. Then she looked at Two Owl. "I'm glad you heard something. I guess I don't have the ears for it." She almost sounded friendly.

The Pawnee looked at her a long moment and said, "Two Owl sorry for what happened back there. When I got rough with you."

She nodded, surprised that she'd gotten what seemed to be a sincere apology.

Two Owl nodded and set off. Night was his friend. Shadow was his twin brother. The tall timber was his protection.

They still made noise, whoever they were, though less noise than they had been making. He pictured where they were and where they were headed. If they continued on their present path they would soon arrive at a spot on the path just below where the two men and the wagon loaded with bank bags sat. He supposed that they had been able to push or pull the wagon back up the hill—whatever was left of it. He also assumed that they were smart enough to figure that somebody was coming after them. The law, or raiding parties, redskin or whiteskin.

He climbed a pine next to the path. The people were headed this way. He would jump them. They would not be expecting him and so there wouldn't be much of a fight. Surprise frequently immobilized people. He had seen even the best fighters freeze up at times and be easy targets for assault.

Two Owl stood on a heavy branch of the tree. Waiting. It would not be long now. It would not be long at all.

"Keep talking."

They were, by the Trailsman's guess, approximately five hundred feet from where somebody of great skill had climbed a tree. He had done it without giving any outward sign of doing so. No shaking boughs, no cracking branches.

An Indian, the Trailsman guessed. Pawnee, most likely. Good fighters, great woodsmen. Fargo doubted that the Pawnee had good intentions. What he was most likely going to do was wait until Fargo and Kate got under the tree where he was hiding and then jump them. Gun or knife, didn't matter. The Pawnee would be skilled with both. He'd most likely choose a gun, though, there being two people he had to capture or kill. The obvious puzzle was what this man had to do with Hack Heller. Could be a complete coincidence but somehow Fargo doubted that. Maybe he'd thrown in with Heller. Heller sure had plenty of money to offer an accomplice, especially one as valuable as a Pawnee brave.

"Keep talking."

"But why?"

"Because you're going to be my cover."

"I am?"

"Yep."

"Where're you going?"

"Up in the air."

"But Skye—"

"Remember. Keep talking. Just like I'm right alongside you. And walk real, real slow."

"I just don't get it."

"We're being watched. From this distance he won't be able to see the trail very well. You'll have to get closer before he can see that there's only you on the trail. It'll help if you walk very slow."

"This doesn't make sense."

"It will," Skye Fargo said. "Just have a little patience."

Fargo had done his share of logging. The dangerous, backbreaking work had been fun for a time because of all the dizzying heights a man got to traverse, jumping from one tree to another. You weren't supposed to do that, of course. But boys will be boys and Skye was all boy. He'd busted his arm a couple of times in the process—spaced reasonably far apart, thank

God—which taught him some respect for what it was like to fall out of a tree. His worst experience was tangling with a wildcat in some hardwoods. He'd lucked out, was able to plunge his knife into the wildcat's heart. The beautiful animal had a long fall to the ground.

He had no problem taking to the trees. He used a long line of them as he would have used stepping stones in a stream. He moved with the same stealth as the Pawnee he was stalking. Several times, he checked the path below him. The way the trees were canopied at this point, no moonlight got through. Meaning that the Pawnee still wouldn't be able to see who was on the path.

The Trailsman moved from tree to tree with fluid skill. The journey was not without a series of minor injuries. Hands, knees, even forehead got barked every once in a while. Several times, pine needles jabbed him in the eye. And once—the scent of sap overwhelming him—he had to clamp his hand over his nose to avoid sneezing. Now there would be a dandy move. All this cat-footed quiet as he made his way to the Pawnee. And then he sneezes.

Four or five trees ahead he saw the murky shape of a human. Fargo stopped. He couldn't go at the man from this angle. The brave would hear him for sure.

He had to move backwards, get several trees behind the Pawnee. That was the best way to ensure surprise.

The problem was time. He had to grab the brave before the brave dropped down on Kate.

He moved now with the same acumen he'd used the night of the wildcat. Became one with shadow, one with branch. The stepping stones. Drawing ever closer to his prey.

He could see the shape of the man more clearly now. The way the Pawnee's body had started to dip toward the path, Fargo could tell that he was preparing himself for his jump.

Four trees separated the men now. Fargo could never reach him in time. There was only one thing he could do and that was announce his presence. Do the opposite of what he'd been doing. Now Fargo wanted to be noisy as hell.

And he *was* noisy as hell.

He rattled the branches, the tree itself. He cracked a couple of jutting boughs. And he said, "Throw down your weapons."

What happened then was what Fargo had wanted to happen. The Pawnee turned around, angry, probably frightened, ready for battle, his gun in hand.

Fargo drew his own gun and started moving toward the Pawnee.

Kate tried to picture what was going on above her in the trees. It was too dark to see, that was for sure.

Apparently, Fargo and somebody else were in a confrontation in the pines. Either that or giant squirrels were hopping from tree to tree. But it couldn't be squirrels because squirrels didn't swear out loud—at least not in English—and squirrels, at least as far as she knew, didn't carry guns. But maybe these were educated squirrels. She knew about the guns because one came falling from the trees and landed at her feet.

The angry battle above went on for a few minutes more. She could picture two men locked in deadly combat. She was amazed—given the way they seemed to be throwing each other around up there—that one of them hadn't lost his balance and fallen to the ground.

And that was when a familiar voice said, "Kate? Is that you?"

Startled, Kate squinted, trying to see into the darkness off the trail to her right. Then Margo and Dave Sadler made it easy for her. They came thrashing out from waist-high undergrowth and stumbled on to the trail in front of her.

Sadler said, "That must be Two Owl up there."

"Who?" Kate said.

"Two Owl," Margo said. "He's showing us where Hack Heller is holed up."

"Well, that's Fargo up there with him then," Kate said.

Sadler sounded grim. "I just want to find Heller. I've been waiting a long time for this."

The trees above them continued to shake with mythic fury. Forest creatures began chittering and chattering.

Then it began raining again. Only this time it was not a rain of moisture, it was a rain of handguns and knives. The fighters above had started dropping their weapons. They must have been in hand-to-hand combat.

And then the two men in the trees came down. Fargo had been in the process of strangling Two Owl and he continued to strangle him all the way down until they both slammed into the unforgiving ground, at which point Fargo's hands fell away from the Pawnee's throat.

Not that the bumps and bruises they'd collected from colliding with the earth had slowed them down any. In moments, both men were on their feet and throwing roundhouses and haymakers and jabs and uppercuts at each other and—despite the dark— mostly connecting.

Sadler managed to put the barrel of his gun against the Pawnee's head and said, "That's enough, gentlemen."

They didn't stop at first but finally they relented after Sadler laid his gun barrel hard against each of their heads in turn.

The two fighters stood three feet apart, their breathing painful to hear—great gory gasps of phlegm, air, pain, unspent rage.

"Skye Fargo," Sadler said, "this is Two Owl. Now you two gentlemen may not have a particularly high level of enthusiasm for working together but Fargo, Two Owl here can lead us to Heller. And Two Owl, Fargo here is about the toughest man I've ever run into. With the two of you helping me, I think we can get Heller without much problem."

Despite all his pain, exhaustion and anger, Fargo was still able to smile inwardly at the tone Sadler had adopted. He was once again the sturdy, professional lawman. The man who was in charge. The man who made the decisions. *Good for him,* Fargo thought.

"How about you two shaking hands?" Kate said—ever the optimist.

"I'm not sure that's a real good idea, Miss Kate," Sadler said. "At least right now. Any kind of physical contact—well, they're liable to start fighting again. It's a nice thought, though." He was just a bit patronizing, the way he spoke to Kate. But lawmen were *supposed* to be just a bit patronizing when they spoke to citizens, so everything was fine.

"Now, I'd like Two Owl to tell us what to expect when we get to the cave up there."

Fargo said, "We can't all go up there."

"Hear us coming," Two Owl said.

"I'm not staying behind again," Margo said.

"Me neither," said Kate.

Sadler said, "I want to kill him as bad as you ladies do. But Fargo's right. We can't all go up there. Let's let Fargo and Two Owl get him and bring him down."

"They'll kill him," Margo snapped. "There won't be anything left for us."

But while they were talking, Fargo and Two Owl slipped away into the night, and began their trek up the hill to the cave. Fargo was content to let Two Owl lead the way. This was Two Owl's land, not Fargo's.

They made no sound as they fled up the hill. They would never be friends, but right now they wanted the same thing, and that made all other considerations moot.

19

Fargo got his first look at the cave about half an hour later. The wagon stood outside. It was ready to go, the bed filled with money sacks, the horses back in harness. The only things missing were Heller and Decker.

Fargo and Two Owl agreed silently, through signs, to split up. The two men wouldn't have left their money behind. They had anticipated an attack of some kind, obviously, and so were hiding, probably somewhere on either side of the cave.

They stayed in the trees, not venturing up to the cave itself. They'd be too easy as targets out in the open that way.

For the next fifteen minutes, Fargo worked his way over to the left side of the hill that contained the cave. Grass that ran to shoulder height in some places grew along this side of the cave. He assumed one or both of the men he was looking for were hiding in it. This location allowed them to see down the hill in front of the cave and also gave them a good look at anybody who might be trying to sneak up the side the way Fargo was.

Even trying to get close to that grassy stretch would get you wounded or maybe even killed. He wondered how Two Owl was doing on the other side of the hill.

Would coming in from that direction be any better? What he needed to know was if there was a man on each side of the cave.

He got his answer not long after he'd started wondering.

Two shots. All he had to go on was the timbre of the voice that screamed out in shock and agony. He was sure that Two Owl had been shot. Maybe even killed. Nobody was invincible, not even a Pawnee brave who knew all about moving up silently on his target.

So there *was* a man on each side of the cave. Fargo would need to take out this one first. Then the other.

He went back into the shallow woods on his side of the cave. He climbed a wide pine tree and started looking for Heller or Decker. It took him some time but he finally saw a movement in the grass—a section moving to the right while the wind moved the rest of it to the left. The shooter, whoever it was, was belly-crawling to the front edge of the grass, which would put him even with the cave mouth.

It took a while for Fargo to figure out why the shooter had moved clear up there, to the path leading uphill to the cave: something was coming up the path.

The grass hid the shooter, and the trees on the other side of the path hid all the activity on the trail. Fargo felt frustrated. Something was going on, but what?

Then he saw her. And he assumed that the shooter did, too.

Margo was crouched down, working her way up the path. She carried her rifle. Easy to figure out what had happened. She'd heard the gunshots and assumed that Fargo or Two Owl was dead. Now she'd turned vigilante. She was—as she'd wanted to all along—going to kill Heller herself. That was her fantasy, anyway.

He had to warn her and there was only one way.

He needed to slip out of this tree and race back down to the path. And he had to hurry. She'd take too many risks. She'd have an explosive thought and then rush the cave. Then she'd be an open target. Either Heller or Decker would kill her on the spot.

He hurried down from the tree. Through the deep grass. Back into the timber on the side of the path. Then a frantic search for Margo.

But she was no longer where she'd been on the path. She had continued to move. She had to be very near the cave now.

Two more shots cracked the black night.

This time he had no trouble deciphering whose scream it was: Margo's.

He rushed to the path and started running up to where she was. Then more shots, close enough that pieces of trunk and bough cut his face as they flew by.

He ducked his head and ran, zigzagging, and grabbed the unconscious Margo's wrist when he got close enough. She was so light it was easy to latch on to her.

He was still ducking bullets. A full minute of rifles blasting away.

He managed to drag her off the trail into the darkness of the trees.

By the time Fargo knelt down next to her, Sadler and Kate arrived, out of breath. "How is she?" Kate said.

"Shoulder," Margo said. "I'll be all right."

But she didn't see what Fargo saw. While Margo might feel the pain in her shoulder, another shot had pierced her chest, just above her heart. She wasn't going to last long if he didn't get her to a doc as soon as possible.

Fargo eased her a bit closer to the trail itself. There was a small break in the tree canopy above them so he could see the wound pretty well. If she was treated by a doc soon, she'd likely be fine. But it had to be soon. He ripped away a section of her shirt so he could apply pressure to the wound itself.

"Kate, I need you to stay here with Margo."

"Maybe you could sing to me," Margo said, her voice weak but sarcastic. She didn't seem to realize how serious the wound was. She was keeping up a show of strength when she didn't have much strength at all.

"C'mon, Sheriff," Fargo said.

"What're we going to do?"

"I'll tell you when we get there."

Fargo had had time to reason through a plan. Since the wagon was already loaded with the bank bags and ready to go, why not take it for a ride?

When they reached the summit of the trail, Fargo said, "I'm going to make a run for that wagon and pull it away from the front of the cave. Watch them come running."

"But you'll get shot."

"That's where you come in. When you see me wave, you open fire just to the left of the cave. That's the only side I'm worried about right now."

"What if they hit you?"

"Then they hit me. There's no other way to smoke them out. And Margo needs to get to a doc as soon as possible."

"You sure about this, Fargo?"

Sadler found out just how sure Fargo was a few minutes later when Fargo topped the hill and the gunfire started coming his way.

Fargo waved.

Sadler, in place, started shooting at a point to the left of the cave. He used his pistol first.

He couldn't believe how well Fargo had thought all this through. Instead of jumping up on the seat and taking the reins, Fargo crouched alongside the team of large horses, leading them away from their post at the cave. But he fitted himself perfectly against the outside horse so that the only way the shooter could get Fargo was to shoot the horse first. Which he most likely wouldn't do.

He heard Heller shout, "Get over here!" So it was Heller to the left, Decker to the right.

In the next few minutes, Fargo led the wagon a good ways from the cave, through the deep, wind-blown grass. Decker joined Heller and they started down the side of the hill so they could start running after Fargo.

Sadler took advantage of Decker's mistake. Decker ran too close to the where the tall grass ended. While Sadler couldn't see the exact shape of Decker, he could see the grass move suddenly and violently. Sadler put three expert shots from his rifle into the thrashing grass. A man screamed. Sadler knew he'd gotten Decker.

Now it was on to Heller. The one he'd been waiting for. He charged into the grass, not worrying about getting shot. He was flush with pride and purpose again.

Heller wasn't exactly quiet. His huge body seemed to trouble and tremble half the earth, with his big feet pounding the ground as he pursued Fargo and the wagon. Sadler must have been making some noise, too, in the tall, reed-like grass. At one point he was forced to throw himself to the ground when Heller turned around and started firing. He couldn't see Sadler but he could hear him. He was obviously hoping to get lucky.

Fargo, hearing the gunfire, started worrying about Sadler. He stopped pulling the team. He yanked his Colt from its holster and started making his way across the clearing where he'd pulled up. He knew the chance he was taking. Heller would be able to see him from the tall grass just ahead but he wouldn't be able to see Heller. Not until it was too late. But he had to risk it to get Margo back to town and the doc. They didn't have much time.

The shot came from the side. Fargo rolled with it so that he could be moving away when the next one came. Two more shots. Then a surprise. One of the shots caught the thumb on his shooting hand. The blood wasn't so bad; the pain was blinding.

He lay on his side in the grass, his good hand clawing around trying to find the gun that had fallen when the bullet ripped through his thumb. In the silence now, he could hear Heller—not exactly a ballet dancer—clumsily tramping through the long grass, looking for the man he probably knew he'd at least injured.

And then Heller appeared, like a wraith emerging from the tall grass—an epic figure looming far above Fargo.

"Hold it right there, Fargo," Heller said. "I ain't done with you yet."

"Need to kill a few more people before you leave with all that money, huh?"

"Things would've gone a whole lot better if you hadn't been around."

"You gonna shoot me, Heller? I'm your kind of target. No gun. No way to defend myself. Just like Jane and Jenna Connolly."

Heller snorted. "They were messing with a good thing. I told 'em both to leave well enough alone. Hell, I even tried to comfort Jane after I killed her sister, but those stubborn bitches just wouldn't listen. Sister Salvation knew it was coming sooner or later, but if their rally turned into a mob, the money would have been gone before I could play my 'part.' Besides, I never figured Jane would try and follow in her sister's footsteps."

But then: "Set it down real slow, Heller. Real slow."

Dave Sadler's voice had a new authority to it. He was hard to see from where Fargo lay—the long grass hid everything—but there was no mistaking his intent. He would be purely delighted to shoot Heller where he stood.

"Well, if it ain't our big, brave lawman."

"Put the gun down, Heller. Now."

"You gonna parade me around town, are you, Dave? Show people that you're in charge again? Then put on a big trial and hang me afterward?"

"The gun, Heller. Now. Or I'll shoot."

While Heller was distracted with Dave Sadler, Fargo eased his hand through the grass. Careful, cunning, like a hunting dog sniffing out prey.

"Maybe you should get yourself a bigger badge now, Dave. Big, shiny one for when you strut up and down the street."

The first thing Fargo's fingers found was a palm-sized rock. Could be handy; could aim for Heller's head. The trouble being that if he missed with the rock, or the rock didn't knock Heller to the ground, Heller was likely to kill him and then Dave Sadler.

He needed his Colt.

"I'm taking three steps closer, Heller," Sadler said. "If I don't hear your gun drop, I'll back-shoot you and not worry about it. You back-shot plenty of men in your time and it don't seem to have bothered you any."

Found it.

The Colt felt powerful—magical—in Fargo's hand. Despite the pain of his thumb, Fargo got his gun ready to fire. He figured that with two guns on him, Heller would have to drop his weapon.

But he was too late.

Without any warning at all, Heller swung around and opened fire on Dave Sadler. Heller couldn't have seen much through the grass and the darkness. But this close to his target, visibility wasn't all that important. Getting off the first few shots was what mattered. But Sadler surprised him by pitching himself—the way a much younger, nimbler man would have—into the deep grass.

Then Heller miscalculated and badly. He swung his gun back to the fallen Fargo and was just about to squeeze off the first of three killing shots when he realized—too late—that Fargo was holding something damn familiar in his hand. The expression on Heller's face turned from sneer to fear as he realized that Fargo had found his Colt and was aiming it right at Heller, just as Heller was starting to squeeze off his own first shot.

But Fargo was one important moment ahead of him. His bullet exploded Heller's forehead. Heller managed to get off two shots but he was falling backwards into the grass and his shots went wild. When he hit the ground, dead, the earth shook as if a giant redwood had been felled.

Just then, breathless from running, Two Owl appeared to see if Fargo was all right.

"You're a little late." Fargo smiled. "But I guess it's the thought that counts."

20

Over the next twenty-four hours, Sheriff Dave Sadler reclaimed his title as the highest law officer in Gladville. He told the bank to pay Two Owl a ten percent reward for its share of the money; made sure that Margo was doing fine at the doc's place; ordered the two deputies he'd just sworn in to see that Sister Salvation had left and to grant her stragglers amnesty; and went and bought himself some new duds, as was only fitting since he was the one, true sheriff once again.

Kate showed up at Fargo's room the next evening. She was bathed, her hair combed out, and smelling fresh and womanly.

Fargo decided to rush downstairs to get them a bottle of good whiskey. He was back in no time.

"That didn't take very long," Kate said as Fargo slid into bed next to her.

"No, it didn't," Fargo said. "But I hope this does."

She said she wanted to make this one special and damn if she didn't. She told Fargo to lie perfectly still on his bed in the darkened hotel room. Then she told him to close his eyes. Then she told him to steady his nerves because he was going to get so excited he might have some kind of heart attack or something. It had been known to happen in situations like this, she giggled.

And then she started by kissing his mouth tenderly while she reached down with a gentle but sure hand and touched the tip of his stiff manhood in a way that made his entire body jerk with joy. "I thought I told you to lie perfectly still," she said.

She then found his mouth with hers. Her tongue made his manhood fill her hand even more. She slowly began to stroke him as she continued to kiss him. Then she began the slow pleasure-torture of kissing him all down his body. Every time he would writhe on the bed, she would take a single finger and push him back into a resting position. She knew what she was doing.

When her mouth reached the tip of him and began to slide down it, he lurched like a wild animal, giving a shout that could probably be heard downstairs.

He forgot everything but the moment and the way she was driving him higher and higher into a state of ecstasy. Forgotten was how they'd thrown Heller's body in the back of the wagon along with the money. Forgotten was how the Sheriff Sadler rounded up Decker and told him to throw down his gun. Decker drew on him. The sheriff drew faster. They threw Decker's body in the back of the wagon, too. Then it was back to town.

While they'd been returning the bank money and tending to a few other obligations, Fargo went over to visit Margo at the doc's office. She was weak, and angry that she hadn't been able to kill Heller herself. But she was definitely on the mend. Fargo cleaned up, ate breakfast, went back to his room and slept. It had been dark when he'd awakened.

In that sleepy darkness, a familiar voice said to him, "A girl could get awful lonely waiting for you to wake up."

And so here they were, her driving him crazy in about the best way he could imagine. But giving as she was—and obviously taking pleasure in that giving—he wanted her to have her fun, too. He moved her head away gently, used his powerful arms to turn her to a sitting position. He sat up on the edge of the bed and then lowered her on to him. When they connected, him up insanely deep, she gave out a gasp accompanied by a shudder he felt through her entire body.

They moved together with interlocking joy. Her narrow hips drove him to a place he'd rarely been before. And she could certainly say the same about the grinding way his powerful hands cupped her buttocks and moved her up and down with such force that her warm, silken juices now ran down both their legs.

And then they were done. It was a mutual climax, too, until they both lay spent on the bed, letting their sweat dry on their bodies, letting their gasping breathing find its natural and much slower rhythm.

All in all, Fargo was feeling pretty good. His thumb was on the mend, and he'd be heading out tomorrow morning. And the short, unhappy reign of Sister Salvation was definitely at an end. He took a long, appreciative look at Kate's perfect body, glistening with sweat from their most recent round of lovemaking.

"You look good enough to eat," Fargo said.

"You know something, Skye?" she laughed. "You do, too."

The Ozark Mountains, 1861—
Where blood kin took on a whole new
meaning . . .

The woman's hands were tied behind her back. Her
face was streaked with grime; her clothes consisted of
a threadbare shirt and britches. A pretty face, Skye
Fargo thought, with bright green eyes and high cheek-
bones and lips like ripe cherries, all framed by lustrous
hair the color of corn silk.

Her captors were cut from the same homespun
cloth, two rough-hewn men with features as rugged as
the Ozark Mountains through which they were making
their determined way. The man in the lead had a
bushy, unkempt brown beard that fell in great tangles

midway to his waist. A double-barreled shotgun rested in the crook of his brawny left arm.

The man bringing up the rear was younger by half, and clean-shaven. He had a rifle trained on the woman's back and was gnawing his lower lip.

Fargo's lake-blue eyes narrowed. By rights this was none of his business. He was passing through northwest Arkansas after spending a wild week in New Orleans indulging his fondness for whiskey, women and cards. The smart thing to do was to keep riding and not interfere. But he found himself gigging the Ovaro into the open and placing his hand on the butt of his Colt. "Howdy, gents."

The bearded man halted and started to raise the shotgun but lowered it again and said in a friendly enough fashion, "Howdy yourself, stranger." His gaze roved from the crown of Fargo's dusty white hat to the tips of Fargo's dusty boots. "We don't often see your kind hereabouts."

"My kind?" Fargo repeated. He was studying the woman, admiring how her hair cascaded over her slender shoulders and the swell of her bosom under her shirt.

"It's plain as warts on a toad that you're not hill folk," the bearded man said. "Those buckskins. That gunbelt you're wearin'. Your horse and rig. You're one of those frontiersmen, or plainsmen, as some call them. What might your name be?"

Fargo told him.

"Bramwell Jackson," the man said with more than a trace of pride. "This here is my boy, Samuel. Don't let his baby face fool you. He can drop a squirrel at two hundred yards with that rifle of his."

Wondering if that was a veiled threat, Fargo nodded at the woman. "And the lady you have trussed up?"

"Is none of your concern," Bramwell flatly declared. "So I'll thank you to rein aside so we can be on our way."

"In these parts," young Samuel Jackson threw in, "folks know better than to stick their nose where it doesn't belong."

Fargo leaned on his saddle horn. "I have the same problem with my nose that you have with your mouth. Suppose you tell me why she's tied up like that? And what you aim to do with her?"

"So much for being sociable," Bramwell said. Snapping the double-barreled shotgun to his shoulder, he thumbed back the double triggers. "You'll oblige us or make your peace with your Maker."

Fargo raised his hands, palms out. All it would take was a twitch of the hill man's finger and he would be blown clean in half. "I'm not looking for trouble, mister."

"Then make yourself scarce," Bramwell advised. "What we're doing with this gal is no more than she has comin' to her. Off you go now, or so help me, I'll turn you into a headless horseman."

Careful not to make any sudden moves, Fargo reined the Ovaro off the trail. The trio filed past, Samuel Jackson covering him with the squirrel gun until they were swallowed by vegetation. The woman never once looked back, never once said a word.

Pushing his hat back on his head, Fargo scratched his hair in puzzlement. He didn't know what to make of it. He should do as the hill man told him and continue west to the Rockies. The woman had not asked for his help. She hadn't so much as looked at him. So why get involved? he asked himself.

Fargo glanced in the direction he had been going, then in the direction the Jacksons and their captive had taken. "When will I learn?" he said, and reined after them. He held the stallion to a walk; he was in no hurry to ride into the twin barrels of that shotgun. There was a common saying to the effect that buckshot meant burying, with good reason. A shotgun was the next best thing to a cannon. It could splatter a man's innards from hell to heaven and back again.

The woods were quiet but that was to be expected. Birds and small animals often fell silent when their domain was invaded by man.

The undergrowth was thick, but by rising in the stirrups Fargo could see almost fifty yards ahead, enough to forewarn him of an ambush.

Evidently the hill men were in a hurry. They quickened their pace and never once looked back. Nor did they speak to the woman, who walked with her chin held high in silent defiance.

The terrain was typical of the Ozark Plateau, as the region was known. Steep hills, verdant valleys, and rapid streams had to be traversed. Hardwood and pine forests were the rule, broken by fertile lowlands layered with rich soil suitable for farming.

Fargo came to a wooded tract of shortleaf pines. Signs of wildlife were abundant, everything from gray and red squirrels to deer. He noticed a log that had been ripped apart by a black bear in search of grubs. A little further on he spooked a rabbit, which bounded off in long, frantic leaps.

Down one hill and up another. That was how Fargo spent the next hour and a half. Then he heard a yell and the murmur of voices. Drawing rein, he slid down and shucked his Henry rifle from its saddle scabbard, and after looping the reins around a handy limb, he cat-footed through the brush until he came to the end of the trees. He thought he would find a homestead. Instead, he beheld an entire settlement.

Over a dozen ramshackle buildings lined a dirt street that ram from south to north. Plank and log buildings cobbled together by someone who never heard of carpentry looked fit to collapse at the next strong gust of wind. A crudely painted sign identified a general store. Another advertised THE JACKSON-VILLE SALOON.

Other than a lone mule at a hitch rail, there were no signs of life. Fargo figured the heat of the afternoon sun had driven most of the inhabitants indoors.

The saloon door opened and out strolled Bramwell Jackson. A much older man accompanied him and produced a plug of tobacco. They each took a bite and chewed, their cheeks bulging, and talked in hushed tones.

Fargo circled to the left to come up on the saloon from behind. He intended to find out what had become of the woman and why she had been bound. Passing a gap between two houses, he spotted her at the other end, on her knees in the dirt, young Sam Jackson standing guard. Sam was staring toward the saloon and kept shifting his weight from one foot to the other.

On an impulse Fargo crept toward them. He made no noise but the woman looked up and saw him. She did not smile. She did not seem relieved. She did not react in any way.

"I want you to know I don't like this much," Sam Jackson said, glancing at his charge. "But since you joined the rebels, I reckon it's fittin'."

"Oh sure," the woman angrily spat. "Blame the women. Isn't that always the way?"

"Don't start with me, Clover," Sam said. "I'm only

doing what I'm told." He let out a long sigh. "You'll be lucky if they let you off with a hundred lashes with a bullwhip."

Clover shifted and glared. "Why don't the elders just up and hang me? They'll have one less worry."

Sam snorted. "You're peculiar, even for a female. Count your blessin's you're still breathin'."

By then Fargo was close enough to touch the Henry's muzzle to the back of Sam Jackson's neck. "Not a peep," he whispered. "Not so much as a twitch." Fargo half expected the young man to shout a warning to Bramwell but Sam stood stock still, his mouth clamped shut. Reaching around, Fargo relieved him of the rifle. "Back up. Nice and slow."

Once Sam was out of sight of the saloon, Fargo made him lie facedown on the ground with his hands behind his back. He removed the younger man's belt and used it to bind Sam's wrists. The belt was old and cracked and wouldn't hold him for long, but Fargo only needed enough time to reach the Ovaro.

Sam broke his silence. "You shouldn't be doing this, mister. You have no idea what you're mixin' into."

"I couldn't just ride off," Fargo said.

"My pa will be furious. So will Grandpa. They'll come after you, mister. Mark my words."

"Let them." Removing his bandanna, Fargo paused. There was something he had to know. "What did this woman do? Is she wanted by the law?"

"No, nothin' like that," Sam said. "She made the mistake of gettin' the leader of our clan good and mad."

"That's all? Open wide," Fargo said, and when the young man obeyed, he stuffed the bandanna into his mouth. "In case you get any ideas about yelling for help."

Sam coughed a few times, then breathed noisily through his nose.

Turning to Clover, Fargo was surprised to find her still on the ground. "I can get you out of here."

"Why should I go with someone I don't know? Someone I never set eyes on until today?"

Her answer was another surprise. "It's either that or the bullwhip," Fargo said, which goaded her into rising and coming over. Bending, he drew his Arkansas toothpick from its ankle sheath inside his right boot and set to work on the rope around her wrists. "What exactly did you do?"

Clover stared at Sam Jackson and did not answer.

"Suit yourself." Fargo wrapped a long piece of rope around Sam's ankles and knotted it. "There. That should buy us the time we need." Taking hold of Clover's warm hand, he hurried into the trees. "Anyplace I can take you?"

"No."

Fargo was growing annoyed with her attitude. "You might at least thank me."

"For what? Being an idiot?"

Fargo stopped and looked at her, but before he could ask her to explain herself, there was a shout from the settlement. Bramwell had found his son and was bellowing for others to come on the run.

"Let's light a shuck." Fargo ran the rest of the way. Vaulting into the saddle, he lowered his arm. "Up you go."

Clover hesitated. "I don't see why you're going to all this bother." But she permitted him to swing her up behind him.

"Hold on," Fargo cautioned, and applied his spurs. They broke from the underbrush and he brought the Ovaro to a gallop. Her arms slid around his waist and clamped tight, her cheek resting on his shoulder blade.

"There they go!" someone hollered.

A shot shattered the tranquil woodland and lead smacked into a tree trunk. Looking back, Fargo glimpsed riders already giving chase. He reined left, threading through the boles with a skill born of long experience. No more shots rang out, and after a while the dull thud of hooves faded. Soon he felt safe in slowing so as not to unduly exhaust the stallion. He glanced at Clover, who had her eyes shut and was scowling. "Are you all right?"

"Never better." Her sarcasm was thick enough to cut with a blunt table knife. "Stop and put me down. I can find my own way from here."

"Not until you tell me what that was all about," Fargo said. A reasonable request, in his estimation, after his efforts on her behalf.

"When goats fly." Clover opened her eyes and straightened. "Fargo, is it? I suppose I should be grateful, but all you've done is brought more grief down on my head. The elders will be madder than ever."

"The who?"

"The elders? They run things. Run Jacksonville. The rest of us must abide by their decisions or else." Clover paused. "Usually."

Although Arkansas was a full-fledged state, parts of it were as wild and wooly as the untamed territories west of the Mississippi River. Federal marshals were too few and too scattered to be counted on, and many counties had yet to appoint sheriffs. Settlements like Jacksonville had to deal with lawbreakers as best they were able.

"Why are they out to punish you?" Fargo asked.

"I spoke my mind," Clover said. "Happy now?"

"Since when is that a crime?" Fargo was listening for sounds of pursuit but so far he had not heard any.

"Since Porter Jackson took it into his head that he's the Almighty," Clover said bitterly. "He founded Jacksonville nigh on twenty years ago, and he lords it over everyone as if it were his God-given right."

Several questions occurred to Fargo, but just then hoofbeats drummed in the distance. Once more he brought the Ovaro to a gallop; once more Clover had to cling tight. She clung so hard, in fact, that he could feel the enticing swell of her breasts against his back.

"You'll never outrun them," Clover said in his ear. "They know this country a heap better than you."

"Maybe so," Fargo acknowledged, "but I won't make it easy for them." So saying, he plunged down one slope and up another, skirting thickets by a hair-breadth, avoiding boulders by a whisker. At the top of the next hill he drew rein and scanned the country-side to their rear.

"Look there!" Clover exclaimed, pointing.

Fargo had already seen them. Six riders, coming hell-bent for leather. In the lead was a burly slab of muscle with a big brown beard.

"Bramwell will never forgive you for shamin' up his son like that," Clover said. "He's right proud of his pups, Sam most of all."

Wheeling the Ovaro, Fargo descended the hill and traveled half a mile to a wooded rise dotted with dead-fall. A game trail offered a way to the top and he took it, expecting another slope on the far side. Instead, he came to a stop at the edge of a bluff over a hundred feet high. Below were jagged rocks and the bleached skeleton of a buck, stubs of its antlers still attached to the skull.

"Is there a way down?" Clover asked.

Fargo leaned as far out as he dared, clinging to the saddle horn with one hand, his right boot nearly out of the stirrup. "Not that I can see."

"That's too bad."

"Don't worry," Fargo assured her. "I'll turn around and we'll be long gone before Bramwell gets here."

Clover put her hands on his shoulders. "No. I meant it's too bad for you. You deserve better after being so nice and all."

"I don't understand," Fargo said. The next moment he did; she shoved him with all her might while simultaneously kicking his right leg free of the stirrup. Before he could so much as blink, he plummeted over the brink.